book! Keep up
the good work
Mrs. Director,

Chip Matty

nobody

To Marilyn,

May God bless
you through the
Gospel Message of
this great work.

Hi Director,
Edward Lalli

nobody
christopher r. mattix

TATE PUBLISHING & *Enterprises*

Nobody
Copyright © 2009 by Christopher R. Mattix. All rights reserved.

No part of this publication may be reproduced, stored in a retrieval system or transmitted in any way by any means, electronic, mechanical, photocopy, recording or otherwise without the prior permission of the author except as provided by USA copyright law.

The opinions expressed by the author are not necessarily those of Tate Publishing, LLC.

Published by Tate Publishing & Enterprises, LLC
127 E. Trade Center Terrace | Mustang, Oklahoma 73064 USA
1.888.361.9473 | www.tatepublishing.com

Tate Publishing is committed to excellence in the publishing industry. The company reflects the philosophy established by the founders, based on Psalm 68:11,
"The Lord gave the word and great was the company of those who published it."

Book design copyright © 2009 by Tate Publishing, LLC. All rights reserved.
Cover design by Kandi Evans
Interior design by Joey Garrett

Published in the United States of America

ISBN: 978-1-60696-670-9
1. Fiction / Action & Adventure
2. Fiction / General
09.03.16

To my parents, Mark and Carol,
And to all who have contributed
To making this dream a reality.
Foremost, I thank God,
He gave me the wings
And taught me how to fly.

Chapter
one

In the pitch black of midnight, the sky seems eerily lighted by the millions of stars of the universe. It feels quite powerful to cover a single star with a finger or a small number of stars with one's whole hand. Have you ever wondered why the stars we see seem blurry and disfigured? Think about it another way: we may visualize the stars as far away and miniscule, but to any star, including the sun, we are not even there. We are but a blip in the aerospace.

The universe seems so very dark from earth. A cold and devastating place, lifeless and hopeless; but there are millions of encircling galaxies surrounding us. There are an infinite number of isolated stars that have been there since the beginning of the world; a huge array of rocky and gaseous planets that continually follow their dreary, methodical order, in one of the many galaxies. The vastness of the universe outside of us, and the gigantic number of heavenly systems, stars, planets, and moons just underline how entirely insignificant the proud human race really is.

"It's the end of the world!" I hear the people scream. Devastating world wars have come and gone, and we are still here. The black plague has been defeated; we have cures for old sicknesses. There are treatments today for some sorts of cancer, and AIDS has not wiped out the entire world—yet. News blurts out the incapacity of the human race to live in harmony, and people slaughter one another without care. The future looks red with the blood of future wars, unbearable sorrow, and devastating natural disasters. But the sun still comes up every morning, although pollution and acid rain may cloud its full glory. The stars still "twinkle" and the moon will always seem to be made of Swiss cheese by some crazed lunatics. And aliens still invade the earth in the sci-fi movies, and UFO's are seen daily on the Mississippi River, where drunken men will imagine anything.

But the rest of the silent universe does not care. Should it? If planet earth erupted into a flaming mass of fire and brimstone, the universe might think better of us: "Orion, *look*!" one star would say to the next, "A shooting star. Quick, make a wish!"

From the cold blackness of space I can barely distinguish a few dots in the view, if I squint very hard. They are spread out thinly, in an oval shape. I take a closer look and see a tiny speck inside of it. There is a star sitting in the middle of the mass, and it evokes most of the light seen in that small area. I strain to put this into view as I pass differently colored circular rocks. Some have rings, some are purple, some are cold, and some have engulfing craters. One of the smallest planets in view is a green and blue ball that swims gently in its space. It has distinguishable shapes on it, one shaped like Popeye's bulging forearm, with the fist down, holding up the largest object on the planet. It might be described as a large kids' bat with a fat end that has just swung and hit a baseball, leaving pieces of dirt flying behind the moving object. It seems to be headed straight into the white glove of a catcher who sits on the bottom of the planet. Or is it the top? As I travel to the opposite side of this oval object, I see two similar objects that look connected by a small piece of green land. It may seem that these two objects reflect the shape of two hurricanes, with the bigger one above constantly whirling and spurting off debris into the nearby blue, but it is hard to see precisely, since the clouds cover most of the vivid colors. This is earth.

    I duck under the cloud cover and go to the lesser of the two hurricanes, South America, to the precise center of it. Here I find the country of Bolivia. On the left of this country there are protruding peaks of different mountains that have pierced the lowest clouds, white with snow. The South is flat and bleak, a light red, and dry as a bone. When I take a look to the Northeast, I see the expanding green of life, with many streams and rivers emerging through the maze of trees and flowing towards the mighty Amazon River and finally emptying into the Atlantic Ocean.

    In the middle of this diverse country there is the third-world city of Santa Cruz de la Sierra—in which well over a million people reside. The main streets circle the city, in huge separated rings connected by long straight streets that divide it into huge pieces, like a gigantic pie. In the Southeastern part of the city, squeezed tightly between the second and third rings from the middle we see the main bus station of the city. A big white and red double-decker bus is leaving the gate and accelerating onto the highway. All the small white cabs screech and honk at the bus as it cuts them off. Black exhaust fills my view, as the bus driver presses hard on the metal below his worn leather boot. He is an old, sour man; his eyes are glowering, black, and without feeling. He cuts off another couple of cabs and a *micro* as he accelerates and moves the stick down into second gear. He didn't get much sleep last night since he had to do a double shift. Yesterday he drove the road from Camiri to Santa Cruz, getting in at one in the morning; and now again at nine he is heading back. His face is disgusting and shriveled, and one side of his mouth is packed with soggy coca leaf. He takes a round-about and then holds his hand out to his helper to hand him some *bicarbonato*.

Opening the compartment door, I enter the long hallway and see rows of double seats on either side until the rear. One lady is arguing about sitting by the window, pointing to the seat number on her ticket and comparing it to the picture of a window by her number. The other person pretends this isn't important, sitting his fat belly on his lap, slowly sipping his bag of lukewarm soda through a plastic straw. A young girl is on her cell phone, making a quick call to her parents to tell them she has gotten on the bus okay, and that she will see them soon. Halfway down the rows I see a young boy with light skin listening to some music on his headphones—a strange sight indeed. A fat woman is across from him, squishing a smaller man against the wall. But he doesn't complain; it is his wife, to his bad fortune. He just grabs the edges of his small sweater and covers himself from the cold air coming through the broken window.

A short, dark-skinned young man comes through the entrance to the hallway with a big sack of papers, and begins selling the daily newspaper, smelling strongly of body odor. The light-skinned boy with the headphones pulls out a few coins and buys a paper. The headline reads, "*Evo Morales Quiere Aprobar la Nueva Constitución.*" It is dated August second. A cartoon picture is painted of the president, giving him big ears, a monstrous nose, and a soccer ball for a brain. He is not very well-liked in these parts of the country.

The atmosphere on the bus is relaxed. The woman who wanted the window seat couldn't get the man to move so she called the helper boy from the cabin and he moved the man to the aisle seat. Many people are huddled in their blankets, with their eyes half closed, trying to find some sleep as the old tires roll on monotonously over the black asphalt. The young *gringo* has stretched out his seat, and has his music blaring to the sound of U2.

A quiet sigh is heard and some eyes stare at the ceiling as an indigenous boy walks into the passenger compartment and begins to sing a song in his high squeaky voice. He appears to be only eleven or twelve years old. The fat woman rolls over and further crushes her hapless husband, trying not to listen to the boy. The small black eyes of the child see the rejection, but he has seen it so many times before that he continues with his song, unabated. The white boy turns the voice of Bono up louder and stares out the window, watching the multitude of appealing signs and vulgar pictures fly by. Everyone knows that the boy will sing his little song and then pass around his dirty brown hat asking for money.

And just so, when the boy finishes his song, he walks down the aisle and all the way back up again, but there is not a cent in his hat. He looks down at it silently and reaches for the door to go out. The same story, again.

His story is the one we will follow. It seems odd that I, as your narrator, would choose the poorest and saddest of all these characters to write about, does it not? Well, answer me this: is it the famous and the rich that merit the most attention? Is it the people who already have a family, a home, or a spouse that need affection? No. It is the invisible people that we need to see—the people begging to be loved, truly, if only for a moment. That is why I invite you to meet Juanito Gutierrez—a nobody.

Chapter Two

Juanito's dirty hands reached for the small door handle. He will be telling the driver to stop and then get off. He will be staying wherever he is left off and hope to find some way of getting back before nightfall to his bed—a bag stuffed with some rag clothes under the bridge on the second ring. His hand clenched the door handle, and his eyes began to water. His first song was all too well known, and no one cared to hear his boring, immature voice. With a strange power he suddenly turned around, forgot the past, and said in a loud voice:

"I'm so very sorry to interrupt you on your trip and bother you as you try and get some rest on the long ride ahead to your destination," It was kind of a rule: people will listen if you use flowery language, so his friends from the streets had told him. "It would be so kind if you would spare me but a minute or two of your time to sing you a tale. It's about a friend of mine. I felt sorry for him and wrote this song about him." The young boy stepped forward a bit more, putting one of his hands on a nearby chair for support. "Here it goes."

Groans and moans came up from the passengers who were entirely relaxed in their seats. But the boy wouldn't be stopped, not today.

"I...was sitting by the chapel, asking any passers by to give me alms. The bells, they began to toll, their song in joyous, joyous sounds of youth. I looked inside the tall church doors and saw a bride, standing arm in arm with her groom." A small pause was made by the voice as he took in a breath to sing the chorus. "It was no other than my mother, in that white dress, before the Holy Cross of Christ. The woman that had given me being had left me on the streets. Forsaken, I walk the streets by night so the sun won't see my tears." Some listeners gazed up uncomfortably as they heard the tragic tale. His eyes were wet with sorrow, and he kept wiping his nose with his raggedy green sweater. Juanito started the second verse, in the same sad note with which he had begun:

"I...live on the streets all day, begging for someone to care for me. My poor soul is crying for love in this broken world we all call home. I would wish upon a star by night, that I could have a mother just like all of you. Like you-u." The faces of all the passengers now showed strained and sad expressions. The fat woman had now leaned into the aisle and was taking in every word. Even the white young man had turned off his music, and even though he still had his headphones on and was pretending to look out the window; he was listening closely to the boy's tale, feeling the pain of the words in his heart. Juanito's eyes had great expression, their blackness, shining in the light, showed a picture of his broken heart. He sniffled and took another big breath, to reach the high notes in the chorus:

"When you see these tears are for real, please pray for me and stretch out your giving hand. For if no one cares, and no one wants to give, my only rest will be in the everlasting arms of God. So forsaken, I will walk the streets by night so the sun won't see my tears."

A very strange thing happened that day. While most passengers usually hoped that their annoying entertainers would hurry up and leave the bus, this time they almost wished he would stay and sing more for them. But Juanito needed to exit before or at the bus' first stop, or else he would have to pay for a full ticket. And it was coming up, so the young boy took off his dirty little hat and began making his way down the aisle again. A smile lit up his face as coin after coin was put in. Halfway down the aisle, where the fat lady had sat so intensely moved by his song, he stopped to ask her if she would put in a coin.

"I don't have much to give you," the obese lady began, and the young boy could see her husband in the corner nodding heavily, as he rolled his eyes at her friendliness with his money. "But have this, and may the *Virgen de Urkupiña* always watch over you ... and your poor, poor friend. Give some of this money to him for me, will you?" Juanito nodded in acknowledgement as she carefully placed a ten *boliviano* note in the hat. The Caucasian boy then turned to the boy and put in a coin. All the way down the aisle the boy went, receiving alms and good will offerings from the passengers. As he was about to exit, he said some grateful words of thanks:

"May God be pleased with this offering you have given today to his grateful child. And may Mother Mary think graciously of you." And so he walked out, as the passengers of the bus began slowly clapping, saying "God bless you, son" and "May the Virgin watch over you," and such Catholic farewells. He walked out and shut the door, telling the driver he was ready to get off. The assistant asked him what the ruckus was about, and he said he didn't really know. The horn went off for the air breaks and the bus slowly came to a halt. He walked off and stood by the roadside as the bus accelerated and began to pass him, as he stood on the asphalt with his hat full of money. People leaned out the window and waved to him as the bus moved on. Tears began to fill his eyes and fall from his cheeks as he began the journey back home.

This is why life is so very beautiful, because our hearts fight to let us embrace inevitable failure, yet to expect the unexpected. For I believe that the vast majority of people in this world survive off of hope, but the people with passion truly live.

Chapter
Three

When one has no friends, no life, and no purpose to pursue a dream, silence becomes your best friend, and the wind's paths are the only arms that will hold tight. But who will love someone who does not even love himself?

A cold and melancholy breeze flew from side to side between the streets of the city, while the multitudes lay silent in their beds, resting peacefully in the safety of their warm blankets. The old man's teeth chattered, as he held his thin body, rubbing his ribs and empty stomach with his hands to keep warm. His long, rumpled, black hair stuck out all over, and by looking closely you could see his brown skin, cracked and wrinkled as it lay on the acute angles of his face.

He stood behind a low shrub that was growing under

the window of a large house. His face was ugly and distorted, and his body was thin and malnourished, but this was not why they called him the crazy man of the neighborhood. His talk was not embarrassing or savage, like the talk of many mad men tends to be. He was childlike and innocent. His behavior was that of a tame dove or a puppy, staying in the corners of buildings and sitting quietly as people looked on. But the children always laughed at him, and men customarily threw water at him, and when drunk, urinated on the man's sickly body. All the women of the neighborhood shielded their children's eyes when they passed by the man, and looked away themselves at the old man's disgrace. What made him the "crazy man" was that he was always nude, and never bothered to cover himself.

A white pick-up slowed down as it approached the area where the old man was crouching. Its tires stopped moving, and a white hand turned the key to kill the engine. He got out carrying a big black bag and made his way over the green grass by the sidewalk to the man. He was Caucasian, young and very tall.

"*Maestro*," he called out to the man sitting timidly behind a plant near a brick wall. "Here, take these clothes," the white man called out over the restless wind, as he pulled his leather jacket tightly around himself. At first the old man was frightened and put his bony arms around his shins and backed further into the corner.

"No, no. I won't hurt you. I have clothes ... they will keep you warm!" the man looked up and showed his dark black eyes, shining in the rising sun. "Clothes," the young man repeated louder. Then he pulled out a sweater and a pair of jeans from the bag. The thin man then slowly stepped toward him and touched the clothes.

"Clothes!" the naked man said, twitching from side to side to see if anyone else was around, and blinking his eyes quickly as he smiled big at his benefactor. He snatched the clothes and backed away, as he sat on the wet grass. He grabbed the clothes and laid them over his freezing body, shivering as he tried to get warm.

Just then, Juanito passed by on the way to visit his father. He was holding his thin green sweater tightly to his body as he walked along. He was confused when he saw a car parked by the road and a white man talking to a naked man. He had seen the poor old man before and had never done anything to harm him—nothing to help him either. As he passed by them, he saw the young man give the other a sweater and a pair of pants. He stopped and looked on from a short distance.

"No, let me put it on for you," the white man said. He walked to the old man and reached for the clothes. Panic filled the man's eyes as he held on tight to the clothes, his bony fingers fighting to hang on to his newest possession. Finally the other man withdrew his gift and told the thin man he would show him how to put on the clothes so he would stay warm. The old man nodded, almost mechanically, without blinking as he watched his gift. He rubbed his hands together and blew warm air on them as he continued to stare, making a strange, laughing smile.

"Mine," the old man said as the other put the sweater carefully over his head. The young man struggled to find the holes for the cold man to put his arms through, and eventually was able to get the sweater on him, bulging around the old man, and reaching near the middle of his scrawny thighs.

"Now the jeans," he called. The crazy man lunged at the faded blue pants and put his right leg into the left hole. Juanito chuckled quietly from the sidewalk as the annoyed foreigner kept telling the man he had them on backwards.

"Uh-hei-hei!" the sickly man laughed in an uncommon, nasal, voice. He proceeded to put his other foot in the same hole he had put the first leg into. He took a tiny step forward and toppled onto his face. He laughed as he turned around and looked at the new friend. He had an innocent laugh, but when blood started coming out of his nose, his laugh turned into pandemonium and fear as he rubbed the blood around his face and then dried his red hands on his new sweater.

"Ah..." the foreigner sighed a few times and closed his eyes for a few seconds before he proceeded to help the frightened man. He got out his handkerchief and cleaned him up, telling him it was all right, and that he had no need to be afraid. He took the pants off the old man and put them on correctly. He helped the old man to his feet and had him hold his oversized pants up. A brilliant smile sparked the crazy man's face just as he let go of the pants and began clapping without rhythm, while making weird noises. The pants fell to the ground, and so the young man picked them back up and told him to hold on to them again. The old man let go once again, and another succession of giggles and laughs followed, as the childish old man clapped at himself again.

Juanito shook his head in humor and continued his walk down the street. The old man would likely be naked again before the day was out. He passed the white car and noticed a large sticker on the car's window; it was an outline of a fish with words inside that read: "*Jesus Salva.*"

Chapter Four

There is something about love,
I dare not say I understand it.
I do not.
There is something about love,
Not sensual,
But heavenly.
How the word has been broken,
Tormented and destroyed.
Love—
To feel an arm around you,
An embrace that takes your breath away,
A joy that lifts you into the clouds.
Yes love, when shared, is beautiful.
A sorrow kept silent is blinding,

Destructive, incessant.
To share sorrow with another—
To watch another's face break down,
To see their tears fall like rain—
That is blessed.
You are loved, wanted, needed.
There truly is something about love,
I don't understand it,
But I know when I feel it.

The iron doors opened slowly, and the scrawny boy slipped through the small opening made by the strong arms of an officer. Juanito said hello to him, respectful of the man wearing a clean green uniform and handling a billyclub; on the right side of his thick belt a machine gun dangled, and a pistol was in a pouch on the other side.

"You don't usually come on Mondays," The officer noted sternly, not even bothering to look at the boy.

"I know. It's my dad's birthday you see, and I wanted to congratulate him." The boy bit his lip, as he let loose the bait.

"Only five minutes, same as usual. Follow me." Juanito nodded and followed the guard through the courtyard. The boy was in the *Palma Sola* prison, one of the cruelest prisons in the country, where his dad was a prisoner. The looming grey walls were covered with barbed wire that shone in the morning sunrays. Juanito followed the stern guard across the courtyard, looking down at his shining black boots as they lifted a trail of dust behind them. His shoes were dirty and broken, letting his toes protrude; the word *Mike* was branded on it instead of *Nike*. The guard closed Juanito into a small room and told him he would send for his father. So he sat down in the small room on a hard wooden chair and stared at the white-washed wall, which was divided by a thick glass wall. He had been here innumerable times before, and knew it would take ten or more minutes for his dad to come, so he just sat there in the hot concrete room, dripping sweat. The temperature in this room never changed, it was always hot, no matter what.

He sighed and put his hands up to his face after a few minutes of waiting. His deep black eyes shone a little in the dim lighting coming from a sixty-watt bulb dangling a few feet from the ceiling. The boy bit his nails, cleaning them with his teeth, subsequently spitting the mud onto the grimy floor. The skin under his eyes was baggy, and dark purple, showing a lack of decent sleep, and his brown face was thin and dry from malnutrition.

In a way, the little boy was a reflection of the naked man that he had come across earlier. They were both so innocent—so helpless. They were both alone, no one cared for them, and no more hope was left in them to move on. The naked man was mocked for not wearing clothes, but Juanito was almost as naked as him, even though he always wore clothing. His raggedy clothes, filthy face, and begging eyes made him a disgrace to common people and a laughingstock to old friends he once had—when he had a family. Yet both had been shown kindness. The old man had been given clothes by an unknown friend, and been cared for in ways he rarely had been before. Juanito had been loved, for once in a very long time, on that bus by a handful of people who took the time to hear *his* song. It was his song in the end.

It was no friend's tale; in fact he had no friend to base a song on if he wanted to.

His only friend was his father, who was stuck in prison. But he was his friend by obligation, by kinship. Even though it was his father who had committed the crime and was held behind bars, Juanito had also been put behind bars, the bars of what his father had left him with—no home, no family, no mother, and no love. His life had been put on hold. His old friends from school had forgotten him without a doubt, and all the little boy could do was remember the good days. Those were the days when his father was at home, when his stepmother had given him food every day, and when he had a real bed to sleep on—even if they had all lived in a one-room house.

   Juanito's mother had died when he was born, and his father had remarried a fine looking young woman a few of years ago. But she was bitter and cruel, and forever at odds with the boy and his drunken father. They had lived in a makeshift shelter in the Plan Tres Mil neighborhood. His stepmother worked as a cleaning lady most of the day, except for coming home at one in the afternoon to make Juanito some lunch. His dad would sit at home watching television most of the day until two or three in the afternoon, then go to work as a taxi driver for a company until eleven or twelve at night. The only time Juanito would ever see his parents together was at noon, and sometimes not until long after he was asleep. He was regularly woken up at midnight by his parent's quarreling, usually about money, and about his dad's drinking and smoking problems, since he usually only brought home ten or twenty Bolivianos a day.

One day Juanito was able to get out of school early in the morning and come straight home. But his dad was not there, as usual. When his mother came home at noon, they both worried until he finally showed up, with twenty-five red bills in his pocket of one hundred Bolivianos each (worth about fifty days wages for the average Bolivian). Juanito's step-mother was shocked, but nevertheless accepted the money. They invited all their neighbors to a party that Friday night, and more than twenty people showed up, staying all night, drinking, dancing, and listening to loud music. Suddenly the police showed up and crashed the party, blasting their red and blue lights through the desolate, muddy streets. But Juanito and his dad were not to be found. He had taken the boy forcibly and they had gone over the neighbor's wall. Eventually both father and son had taken a cab to a motel where they had planned to spend the night. But the police had found them, broken the door, and shot Juanito's father in the leg. They opened up a bag he had been carrying—it was full of cocaine. Juanito would never forget this night, even if everything had happened in a flash.

Juanito was left on the streets after the police kicked him out of his father's cell. He was sent to an orphanage, but when he escaped, he began doing any job to get money—washing windshields at stoplights, singing on buses, selling magazines, shining shoes, begging for money at the church doors of the Plaza, and stealing. But every once in awhile he was caught and sent back to the orphanage, and then he would escape back onto the cold streets. Yet what did the streets have to offer that the orphanage did not? The orphanage was a good place, a secure place, but it had become a prison to Juanito. He left to obtain freedom, to do what he wanted whenever he wanted, even if it meant sleeping under bridges in the chilling wind, dreaming anxiously about his next meal.

Juanito especially remembered one night; he was walking through his neighborhood by coincidence and spotted his stepmother dancing in a bar. She was next to a tall, dark-skinned man—his arms and chest bulging, and full of muscle. He took her by the arm out of the bar and they headed down the road. He followed them and saw them enter his old house, built-up with an extra room next to it, all painted a clean white. He stood outside the door, holding his hand up to the door as if to knock, but then he pulled his hand away and sat down on the steps outside, as tears fell from his eyes. When the boy had first been let out of the prison, his father sent him to his old house to live there, but his stepmother wouldn't let him in, barring the door and telling him she didn't know who he was. And nothing had changed since that night.

Three years had passed since he had left his house, and he was now twelve years old. Juanito had become his father's slave, working day and night to get money to pay for his dad's bad habits, coming every Saturday night to bring him most of what he had earned. But this was a Monday, and the boy wasn't quite sure why he needed to to be there, but his father had told him to come back because he had found some well-paying work for his son.

Juanito ran his small hands through his coarse, black hair, which was long and growing out at different lengths. Many times he had cut his hair himself with a pair of scissors, which he had stolen. He was bored of waiting.

Finally, when Juanito's rear end had begun to tense up and his seat had become uncomfortable, the door on the other end of the room opened and an officer showed in a fat man in his mid-forties. His face was shaved and clean, but his hair was sticking out, and his eyes were drooping from having just woken up. It was his father. He sat on the chair opposite his boy and frowned through his tiredness. Juanito smiled big and began speaking into the greasy black phone that he picked up from the table. He put his hand to the glass and looked into his father's eyes.

Chapter
Five

The wind blew fiercely through the streets as Juanito squinted and pressed on. Although it was very cold, he didn't feel it because he was wearing a new jacket that was red, and as warm as its color. He had a black cap on his head, and a new pair of jeans on. A large blue backpack was tightly fastened on his back, partly filled with a few food items, an extra shirt, and a bit of money.

It was about midnight, and although it was a working day's night, all the lights on the long *Cañoto* Street were blazing, and people were flooding in and out of various bars and chicken restaurants. Juanito made his way shyly into a noisy chicken restaurant and looked around. A strong smell of liquor filled the room, mixed with the crispy-rich smell of chicken, deep-fat-fried in dirty oil and served on greasy plates that had only been washed in murky, cold water. There must have been thirty or so men in the room, and all of them were staring intently at the huge television sitting in a corner. The large screen flashed out fighting and kung-fu action as Jet Li did his amazing stunts inside the plasma wall, hitting everything in sight, breaking jaws, elbowing a man behind him then punching the man in front, all this while doing his special hand positions and yelling out painful screams of victory. Everyone sat or stood in silence, intently watching the movie, immersing their minds with the "thick" plot.

Juanito carefully observed all the faces he could see from a distance. He went up to the wall of bodies impeding his passage into the center of the room and tried to shove through, but no one moved. He asked politely to be given space, but no one heard him, as his voice was much too soft to be heard over the intense commotion of the television.

"Excuse me!" Juanito said as loud as he could, but still no one moved. This time the men in front of him had heard him, but didn't turn around or even blink an eye. Finally the small boy got up on his tip-toes and beat his hand on a man's back. The man turned around, showing his solemn face and a week-old beard. "Can you let me through? I'm trying to find some men. They are called Guillermo and Lucho," the innocent child said as he caught the man's attention. The man in turn nudged the men ahead of him to make a little room for the boy to go through. All the while, Juanito kept on nodding and saying thank you to the men he passed. Some men mumbled in return as he went by, spreading their thick beer-stained breath over his body.

"Guillermo and Lucho, does anyone know them?" the boy asked a people nearby. He was now in the center of the room, a dozen feet from the blaring television. There were five or six tables sitting in the middle, and on them and around them sat multiple beer bottles. Some drunken men were sprawled out on their chairs, their fat bellies lying heavily on their laps.

"The men you are seeking are over there, son." A slim old man said, in a flowery but slurred tone, as if he were pretending to be an educated man, maybe a prince or a president. He pointed over to two men a few tables away, with his bony hand outstretched, palm up, and signaling with the two first fingers of his right hand. Drunk to the bone would be a good way to describe him, and a few beers short of being mentally retarded would be another. Juanito thanked him with a fake smile as he held his breath and moved away from him.

The noise in the room became unbearable as he got closer to Guillermo and Lucho, since they were sitting right next to the screen.

"Are you Lucho?" Juanito asked, almost screaming.

"No, I'm Guillermo. Get out of the view of the *tele*, before I knock you down, you bastard." He was a small, stout man in his mid-thirties, but already he was going bald and his thin black hair on top had already receded past the mark of his ears and joined the bald spot on his crown.

"Juan, my father... sent me to find you... He said you had work for me." Juanito had to keep taking big breaths to scream out his message.

"Oh, Juan, sure; you're his son?" the grumpy man asked as he held up a chicken leg and bit into it, chewing with an open mouth. Juanito nodded in response. "Juan is an animal; he left us out to dry. We were supposed to leave this afternoon on a … Paraguay." The noise of the movie had made it hard for Juanito to hear the guy.

"What did you say? Paraguay?" Juanito yelled, as he took a seat opposite the man. Meanwhile Guillermo had put down his chicken leg and proceeded to wake up his partner, Lucho, who was sleeping soundly, oblivious to the boom box blaring just inches from his ears.

"Yeah. We're going to Paraguay tomorrow … no, wait …" The man looked down at his watch to see what day it was and then continued talking as half-masticated food fell out of his mouth and onto his shirt, "Today. It's 12:15, so today, in the afternoon," the man sat back on his chair and picked his teeth with his dirty fingernails as he turned his attention back to the movie, "Now shut up, get some chicken to eat and shut up." He took out a bill from his pocket and gave it to the boy, pointing to the counter where he could get some food.

Juanito got up from his seat, made his way through the maze of people in the filthy restaurant and went up to the counter to ask for some chicken. He handed the oriental waiter the bill, and after waiting awhile, received a plate of hot chicken. He took it and went back to the table. Lucho was now awake, his eyes squinting to keep out the light as his face stretched into odd shapes and his lips curled as he yawned long and loud, showing his missing teeth mixed with some gold jewelry stuck in the back like an old car, fixed with duck tape. He was an obese man, with a round face, a triple-decked neck and a double chin. He rubbed his eyes with his light brown hands and then combed them through his hair as he yawned again.

"Who the devil are you?" He asked Juanito as he yelled in his squeaky voice, as he shifted in his chair— and it complained.

"Juanito," the boy said, but the other man looked puzzled so he explained, "Juan's kid. Here to work for you guys." The large man nodded as more folds of fat formed below his chin.

"Here to do the job in Paraguay, I see. Your father is such a son of a…" he felt aggravated, but he held his tongue for the boy's sake. "We should already be halfway to Paraguay by now… but oh well. It's okay; I needed a few drinks anyhow before the long road ahead."

"Are we going to live there in Paraguay? How long are we staying?" the boy asked, hesitatingly, because all his father had told him was that he was going off to a foreign country and he should buy some warm clothes for the long journey. He didn't mention how long he would stay; in fact, he didn't mention if he would be coming back. His father had given him the money to buy the new clothes, the backpack, and the food.

"No, no. We'll be right back in a few days. We'll go down there with our supplies and trade them at the border for the supplies that a contact of ours will bring up from Asuncion, the capital. Real easy, no hassle, and there is a whole lot of money involved too," Guillermo belted back.

"Shut up! *Idiotas*." said a man from across the room, as he tried to watch the movie. There had been a long, boring part of talking in the movie and nobody cared, but suddenly it had burst into action, and Jet Li was back on his feet, doing what he knows how to do best.

"It's not illegal, is it?" Juanito asked over the sound of breaking bones and karate moves.

"Oh no, of course not! Now sit down and eat that chicken in silence so I can watch the movie," Guillermo replied, while Lucho chuckled.

Juanito sat there a few hours, watching the screen, and his charcoal black eyes became sore and heavy, tearing from the brightness. His mouth fell open and it drooled as he became mesmerized by the different movies that were put on. Finally, tired out by the plethora of noises and sights, he got comfortable enough on his metal chair and fell asleep. Eventually he dropped to the ground and curled up there, grabbing his knees because of the cold.

It was the first day of his new life.

Chapter
Six

"Here boy, take this," Lucho said as he launched a heavy box onto Juanito's relaxed body. A loud thump followed as the small boy fell hard onto the asphalt. The brown box he had been thrown pelted off his chest and tumbled onto the ground, under the bus nearby.

"Idiot! What did you do?" asked Guillermo as he ran over to the bus and got on his knees. He carefully grabbed the box, brushed off the dirt and checked that it wasn't broken. "You better not be playing with me Lucho!" He helped a dazed Juanito up off the ground and asked him if he was all right. The boy rubbed his eyes, tears welling up in them. He sniffled and grabbed his sore arm as he nodded.

"Stupid little kid can't even hold a box, I mean come

on Guille, be serious, he can't go with us; we'll be in danger..." Lucho said, chuckling a little to himself, but the balding man wasn't finding any of it humorous. He pulled the fat man aside and shaped him up.

"Shut up, shut up, shut up!" Guillermo said, as he menacingly waved his finger in Lucho's face. He grabbed his arm and led him behind the bus, quietly whispering so no one could hear. Juanito stood at a distance, trying to decipher what they were talking about. Both men argued back and forth for a while, until Guillermo lightly slapped the fat man's face and stared him down, his other hand tightly around the box. Suddenly there was a roaring sound that came from the front of the bus as the old diesel engine came to life, and in effect a large cloud of black smoke came out its exhaust pipe. Guillermo and Lucho ran out from behind the bus, coughing loudly, and lined up to board.

"Are we leaving now?" Juanito asked loudly over the roar of the bus. People began streaming on, pushing and shoving their way through the open door.

"Sure thing, bud, go on in," the thinner man said, pointing to the door in the front of the bus. Once the boy was on, Guillermo grabbed Lucho by the collar of his red polo and pulled Lucho close: "You'd better shut your mouth, *compadre*! I'll kill you myself if I see you fooling around again...maniac!" He pushed him away and forced his way onto the stairs of the bus.

"Yes, sir!" Lucho said after him, in a high-pitched sarcastic voice—the voice of a blond cheerleader may give the right idea. He fixed his collar and heaved his rotund body onto the bus, pushing a lady and her kid back. The bus swayed a little as he boarded.

Once inside the bus, Juanito walked down the narrow aisle as he looked up at the numbers on the sides, looking for his—this time as a passenger, not a beggar. He squeezed past a light-skinned man and sat next to him on the window seat, under number seventeen. He put his face close to the window and looked out at the people roaming the street. He recognized many of the vendors there. One of his friends, a tall, dark-haired boy, was just then making his way alongside the bus, with a small basin filled with *empanadas*, covered with chalky white cream. Juanito waved at the boy and made signs to him, but his friend didn't see him. He opened up his window and called out to the boy, but he still didn't hear him; so after yelling for a bit, Juanito just sat back down and relaxed.

"Excuse me, sir," Guillermo said to the white man sitting next to the boy. He held the brown box over the man and handed it to Juanito: "Here, son. Take the box and put it under the seat."

"It doesn't fit," retorted Juanito, after trying for a while to fit the box under the seat in front of him without success.

"Here," interrupted his neighbor, "I can put it up on top." He reached for the box, but a jumpy Guillermo stood up from the seat he had taken just behind them.

"No, no … It fits, I'm sure it does; just right down there, under your seat, not under the seat in front of you." After saying this, the thin man began making his way back to his seat.

"What's in the box, sir?" Juanito questioned in interest, shaking the box a little.

"Uh. No, nothing … I mean, nothing *very* important.

Just breakable items we are taking with us." Guillermo replied, in an unsure tone.

"It's to sell in Paraguay, right?" Juanito inquired again.

"Yeah. Of course." The thin man answered. Lucho, who was sitting next to him, nudged Guillermo in the ribs and raised his eyebrows emphasizing: *What was I just telling you?*

"Could I see what you are selling, I might be interested." The Caucasian man butted in again, as the bus slowly began to move.

"No ... Sorry, I mean, we already have a buyer. Thanks anyway," Lucho answered quickly from the back seat.

Juanito eventually got the box situated properly under his seat with the help of his friendly seatmate.

"My name's Jesse," the white man said after a long yawn, stretching out his hand to the young boy, "We're going to be on here for about a day, so it would be good to meet."

"Juanito," The little boy answered him, a little shyly, as he took his big pale hand.

"Nice weather today," Jesse said, after a little pause, "Great for traveling, not too cold, not too hot. And we are on the shady side, at least until tomorrow morning." Juanito nodded, as the conversation got off to a slow start.

They talked a bit more, but no real intrigue formed. A half hour later, the tired boy's heavy eyes closed and he fell asleep.

Chapter Seven

Juanito woke up in a pool of sweat, opening his eyes only to be blinded by the scorching sun. It was sometime mid-morning and the whole bus was filled with blistering heat.

"Come sit down here, Juanito," Guillermo suggested. He was sitting in the middle of the aisle, with his knees to his chest, just like a dozen other people down the line. The white man scooted farther forward and made room behind him for the boy. At that time of the day they were bathed in sunshine bursting through the open windows. The air rushing through the open window brought in heat instead of relief, working more like a hair-dryer than a fan.

"Oh...okay." Juanito gave out a long yawn and

rubbed his dreary eyes as he stared out the window. He was looking at the Gran Chaco Desert, but it is not a sand desert as you might expect, instead it is a shrub forest desert, covered with millions of small thorny trees, all tangled and forbidding. There are also various rock protrusions and gullies in various places. Although the desert is owned by rattlesnakes and scavenger birds, the most intrusive and ever-present sight is the *carawata*. This is a plant that is about the size of a basketball and is shaped like a star with many long claw-like thorns, protruding from each one of its thick blades. If you walk through there it will ultimately tear your clothes, and destroy your skin. It was about these plants that Jesse, the Caucasian man, was talking about when Juanito sat down:

"There is this comic story about a missionary about fifty years ago that worked with the Ayoreo Indians in Yanaigua, near the Paraguayan border. They say this missionary had received some money from the United States to buy clothes for these Indians. So he went out and bought a bundle of new jeans for the men, since they weren't used to wearing clothing most of the time," Jesse narrated, and he stopped for a sip of water.

Juanito was now comfortable in the aisle, leaning his back against Guillermo's shins. The American then continued, "So this missionary picked up about a dozen of these Indian men and gave them each a pair of pants. Then he drove the Indians to Camiri, a small town a day's trip away, for the first time in their lives. Well, it just so happened, that a herd of wild pigs crossed the road as they approached, and so the missionary began to slow down and wait for all of them to cross. But before he stopped, all of the men in back got out of the truck and ran through the carawata's after the pigs with their beautiful new jeans on. They returned smiling, carrying two pigs on poles. But the missionary was not pleased seeing their new jeans all torn to shreds," All the people in the bus began to laugh at the crazy story. But Jesse wasn't done.

"But even though their jeans were shredded, their skin hadn't broken open or started bleeding. Their hide was tougher than jeans, even tougher than leather."

"There aren't any naked Indians running around anymore!" Lucho said, shifting his huge body back and forth on the floor, bothering the people around him.

"Well this thing happened about half a century ago, and back then most Indians never wore clothes. But even nowadays I've heard of some Indians in the jungle up north that still wear little to no clothing."

"People are very civilized down here now, though. I've been out to one of the *haciendas* and they have cable TV, cell phones, internet... you name it." A man sitting up on a seat next to Jesse added.

"Yeah, you're right. It's all hotwired. They stick a wire on a tall tree or put a long pole down and tie the wire to it. They use diesel or gasoline generators and sometimes solar panels to provide electricity for the ranch. It's pretty amazing."

"I met a truck driver the other day who had a satellite phone connected to his truck. He said it had cost him an arm and a leg, but said he can now make calls to anywhere in the world for free," the man replied. Then the white man lit up and remembered another story:

"There are some pretty cool gadgets you can buy

nowadays. But there are just certain things we can't control, certain creatures that run off instinct, because God made it that way."

"What are those things?" Juanito asked shyly, now fully awake.

"*Jucumari*, they are called." Jesse answered.

An old woman turned around and added to the conversation, "Sure, I've heard of them. It's a man that has the body and strength of a bear. You can tell by his feet they say. He walks on four feet, but when he runs he gets up on two. And he leaves human looking footprints, five toes on each foot...it looks just like a human, except it's a little wider. It's obviously a myth."

"You're on the right track. But it's not a myth," Jesse explained, "It's a mountain bear that is actually quite harmless if not bothered. It always walks on all four feet, but it does have paws that look just like human feet." Jesse was rudely interrupted by Lucho:

"Now that's a bunch of nonsense, did you get that story out of the same place you got your last story—a children's book?" Jesse then reached up and took off his hat.

"Do you see these long scratches here on my hat?" He turned around so Lucho could see them. There were three large grooves of what looked to be from huge claws. The Caucasian man continued, "This was from the Jucumari in the zoo in Santa Cruz. I put my hat close to the bear and he almost ripped it up. I've not only seen one in the zoo, mind you. I've also seen a Jucumari in the wild."

"Does it eat people?" Juanito asked, his fear clearly noted.

"Of course, it especially loves to eat young boys like you!" Lucho said, sarcastically. Juanito looked over at Jesse with fright in his eyes.

"Not usually. They are shy animals, like I said," the white man reassured, "But if you bother them, they will harm you. They are very territorial and they will throw sticks and rocks at you with their human-like paws. But don't worry, these animals are rare and only live up in the mountains, quite a ways off from here."

It was about two o'clock in the afternoon, of the same day, and the sun had now shifted to the other side of the bus, so Juanito and his seatmate were back in place. The movie on the two little screens of the bus had ended, and some of the passengers up front were begging the assistant to put another one on.

"How do you know so much about Bolivia, when you aren't even a Bolivian yourself? Or are you?" Juanito asked. Jesse looked over from the book he was reading and answered:

"I was born in Bolivia, but my parents are American. They came down here as missionaries more than thirty years ago. I came back down to Bolivia, after college in the United States, to be a missionary here with my wife and kids. I live in Camiri—we passed the town about five hours after leaving Santa Cruz." Juanito nodded.

"Why would you want to be a missionary and live in Bolivia?" The boy asked with wonder.

"Sure Bolivia's poor and people can't find work, and we have a corrupt government... but I didn't come to

Bolivia to make money, or to have all the luxuries I could've had. I came down here because I know there is something more to life than just working, eating, or sleeping," Jesse took a long swig of water and offered some to the boy before continuing. "Most people only live on earth sixty, maybe a hundred years at the most. But after that, what is there?"

"Oh, so are you some sort of a Catholic priest? Because when I was younger I used to go to the Cathedral and hear a priest talk about heaven and hell. Then I had to fulfill certain requirements to be accepted into heaven. But if I didn't fulfill them all I would stay in purgatory until I had finished my punishment. I never understood it."

"Nope, I'm not a Catholic priest. I'm an Evangelical, a Christian. Jesus, God's son, died for your sins and he wants to let you into heaven for free. I have come to learn that while they do care about men's souls to some extent, the Catholic Church, runs a very good money-making business that tries to make you believe that you need to pay for something that was given to you for free. All you need to do is accept the gift that has been given…" The white man was harshly cut off by Guillermo's sharp voice.

"Hey, stop talking all that nonsense and watch the movie, can you?" Guillermo crossed his thin arms and put a frown on his face as he watched the second movie the assistant had put on. Jesse took another swig of water and then reached down into his bag. He pulled out a small sheet of paper that was neatly folded in half and gave it to Juanito.

"Here take this. If you want to know more about

what I was talking to you about, go ahead and read this." Juanito thanked the man for the gift and stuck the folded paper into his backpack. That piece of paper would be lost for many months at the bottom of his bag.

"What is that, *quick*, what is that?" Juanito asked loudly, pointing out the window. About an hour had passed since he had last spoken. Jesse looked up from his book and saw what the boy was talking about and began to explain, without closing his book, *The Heavenly Man*. There was a white cross, about four feet tall standing by the side of the road, with the inscription "*MURIO DE SED*" on it. Around the base of it there was a pile of glass and plastic water bottles that were filled with putrid, moldy water.

"People leave water bottles at the base of that cross to show their sympathy for the people who die out here regularly from a lack of water. Either they get lost and can't find the road again, or they get injured out in the wild and have no one to help them." Juanito stuck his head out the window to follow the cross into the dust. The American man then gave an important word of advice, "You must always travel with someone else when you go out into the Chaco. It is *very* dangerous." Then he resumed his reading.

Chapter
Eight

The hours passed, and the young boy's mind zoomed in and out of outer space, as the bus trudged on through desert with a cloud of black smoke following them all the way to Asunción.

"We made it!" Juanito pronounced showing all the excitement that all the mature adults felt but didn't dare express. Jesse awoke from a light sleep and rubbed his eyes.

"You say what?" he mumbled.

"We're in Asunción." The boy repeated as he looked out the window at the modern cars mixed in with the crowded minibuses that inhaled second hand smoke from the buses ahead of them. He stuck his head out the window for a breath of the city air and his eyes sparkled as he looked at all the people, busily walking to and fro, following their cyclical routines. The boy waved at a lady that happened to glance up at him in the bus. The city was alive with sprouting flowers, budding trees, spotted butterflies, and, of course, the ever-present mosquitoes.

"Come on Juanito, get your things! The bus station is right ahead." Lucho growled as he got up and reached his flabby arms into the overhead compartment for his bag. With all the perspiring he had done on the trip, which you could still see on his shirt, you could almost swear he had lost at least a few pounds.

"Okay," he stood up, all four and a half feet of him, and tried to get by his dozing neighbor, "Mister, excuse me please... Mister! I need to get my bags."

"What? Oh... right, right. Go right ahead." He moved an inch to his side and then closed his dreary eyes again.

"Mister..." But Juanito gave up and just climbed over the man.

"Boy, aren't you forgetting something?" Guillermo's commanding voice warned. Juanito looked back to see his backpack sitting on the floor:

"Oh, wow. Thanks. I really don't want to loose that backpack, it's the one my dad gave me for my last birthday." Juanito crawled over the sleeping white man again and retrieved his backpack as he turned to go back out.

"The box, get the box, idiot!" Lucho yelled. The bus turned into the station and jolted from side to side as it went over a speed bump, throwing the boy's body on to his neighbor's chest.

"I'm sorry, sir." Juanito got off of Jesse as he awoke slightly and looked about him to find he was now in the terminal.

"We're here, finally!" he said, "I thought we'd never make it. It sure went by quick…just a minute ago we were passing Mariscal."

"That was a long time ago, Mister," The young boy answered as he picked up the heavy box from the floor and moved into the aisle.

The two men, the first being the overweight Lucho, closely trailed by the short Guillermo with his thinning black hair flying behind him, and followed closely by Juanito, got off the bus before everyone else. Juanito had to run to keep up with the two men as they quickly made their way into the terminal.

"What are we going to do here? Are we going to work in some shop?" Juanito asked, a little breathless after following them all the way into the terminal. They stopped at a desk and Guillermo pulled out his wallet:

"Three tickets to Ciudad Del Este, please." The attendant smiled back and asked in response:

"There is a bus leaving in thirty minutes, and another one tonight at nine. Which one would you like?" A huge smile broke on Lucho's face as he in turn answered for the group:

"We'll take the one in half an hour. That will be *perfect*."

"No. One second." Guillermo grabbed Lucho by the arm and pulled him aside.

"I thought we were staying here!" Juanito said, completely confused and exhausted.

"Give us a second okay, bud?" The friendlier man replied as he began a hushed conversation with Lucho:

"Look, *compadre*, we've been on that bus from Santa Cruz for almost a whole day, and the kid needs a break.

Let's take him to a little park, have some supper and then come and take the night bus. I'm tired out and I need to stretch…"

"Are you kidding me? The delivery is tonight, at the latest at two. Who knows when the bus gets into Ciudad Del Este? But all I know is that we *need* to be on time, or else they'll skin us alive."

"I guess you're right, Lucho." He spoke up now and to the assistant, "Three seats for the afternoon bus. One for the boy by the window, and two seats right behind him…"

This was just the beginning of a new life for the fragile young boy. He never knew what he was getting into and never even had a choice. For his father it was for the best, but for him it would be for the worst.

Chapter
Nine

"Saint Moses! I'm out of toilet-paper," Lucho said, scrounging around in the small bathroom of the hotel room. He poked his pudgy head out of the door into the dimly lit room and looked around for some paper: "Juanito, check in the drawers of one of those bedside desks. There should be a Gideon's Bible in there." Sure enough, Juanito found a Bible, and began taking it to Lucho in the bathroom.

Ten months had passed since their first trip to Paraguay. All the trips were the same, they would take a bus to Ciudad Del Este, and then with the money they made selling cocaine, they would buy a car and stuff it full of electronics. They would cross over the border again, with all legal items, and reach Santa Cruz where they would sell the items for a higher price to make even more profit. Every trip would give one-hundred percent profit. Then they would stay at a dumpy little hotel near the terminal for a week or two until they got some more merchandise. Their room was a cramped room with one double bed, a television, a telephone, a bathroom and shower, and a balcony. Guillermo would stretch out some quilts on the floor and put Juanito there.

On every visit to Santa Cruz, Juanito would visit his father and give him most of the money that Guillermo gave him for pay. In time, the boy found out that he was working with crooks and selling cocaine. He had been sold, in a way, into a world he did not belong and did not want to belong to. Yet his voice meant nothing, he was the guinea-pig of the operation and a slave to his father's whim.

"You're an animal!" Guillermo yelled across his room after hearing Lucho's comment. He grabbed the Bible out of the obedient boy's hands and looked at it. His face cringed as he looked at its cover. He opened it up and carefully leafed through each page. He reached for the controller and turned off the television he had been watching which had a reporter in La Paz, talking about all the wild things happening under President Evo Morales. Guillermo got up, walked up to the closed door of the bathroom and spoke loudly so that his companion could hear him, "This is a Bible, it's holy…"

"You believe that trash? People say it was written by God. Whatever! Have you ever seen God? I don't think so." Lucho retorted, from behind the closed door.

"That's what you call faith. Everyone has faith in something. It's not that I don't believe in God, but I don't want to commit myself to him either, it's too hard." The skinny man said, scratching his forehead uneasily, as he turned back and sat on the side of the spring-bed that cried loudly on impact.

"It probably doesn't help you much being a criminal!" Lucho said, and you could hear him laughing loudly, "You aren't gonna get very high up the ladder of heaven." He continued laughing, but Guillermo was already quickly looking through the book for a verse.

"For God so loved the world, that he gave his only... be... go... tt'n... begotten Son that whosoever believeth in him should not perish, but have everlasting life." The thin man looked down carefully and kept on reading intently the rest John 3 to himself. "I really don't understand how Jesus would give us salvation for free. It means we don't have to do anything..."

"Thank you, *Pastor Guillermo*, for that beautiful moment of reflection. That's a bunch of horse dump! Just like the place were in. No toilet paper, are you kidding me?" There was silence for a while until the overweight man turned on the shower. The clatter of waterdrops falling to the ground downed out every other sound and made the thin man look intently at the floor as he closed the Bible and set it beside him on the bed. Juanito noticed sadness in the man's eyes, and he could almost decipher a forgotten tear welling up in them. The young boy sat on the floor in the corner, on the blankets that Guillermo had set down for him. He looked out the window to see the red setting sun as a mood of loneliness fell over his young shoulders.

"Guillermo?" the boy asked quietly, while still staring out the window. The man was startled for a bit, but answered calmly,

"Hey bud. I forgot you were sitting there. You haven't said much. What did you want?"

"Did you used to be a Christian?" the thin boy asked, as his dark skin shone in the dying sunlight.

"Sort of. I fell in love with this pretty girl, Ana, at church, and I couldn't take my mind off of her. So I pretended to become a Christian, and said I attended a church in another part of town. I went to that church for a year before they found me out. Everyone liked me, I even led the singing a few times…" his naturally strong voice sunk into a mere murmur as he continued, laying back onto the bed and looking at the ceiling. His face was getting wrinkles and his hair was falling out, and everyday Guillermo knew he was growing older and older, "All I wanted was to get married and have a few kids and a home. If only I hadn't…" Guillermo stopped talking for awhile and made the boy impatient so he asked,

"What did you do?" A tear that Juanito couldn't see fell down the face of the broken man.

"I was a cab driver for seven years. Every once in a while there would be a party… and I was invited to a friend's party one night. I intended not to get drunk, but I got absolutely stoned. An elder from the church saw me on that occasion and that was the end of my relationship with Ana." He paused and let a few more tears drain from his heart as he regained his poise, "I was going to be baptized that Sunday, then I had planned to take her out to supper that night and ask her to…" he paused once more and this time Juanito could hear the quiet sobbing. He sniffled and finished up: "Marry me."

He sat up and rubbed his reddened eyes, not wanting to look into the eyes of the young boy. "Now I'm a drug-dealer, a criminal and a wretched bastard!" he now stared into the shiny eyes of the boy: "And now I've gotten you into this as well. I promise Juanito, I will do everything I can to get you out of this dreadful mess." The man lowered his head and shook it slowly back and forth with his eyes closed.

The water in the shower stopped running and normality returned as Guillermo's face again turned to stone.

"We're going to go down to a bar tonight and talk with some men that are going to help us in our work. You don't have to go to see your dad or anything do you?" Guillermo said in his potent voice.

"No. No. Nothing." Juanito said, trying to keep a straight face, but the thin man noticed a problem and didn't let it pass:

"What? Tell me boy, don't be afraid."

"It's my birthday tomorrow." Juanito said, looking at his bare feet.

"What? It's your birthday!" Lucho said, walking out of the shower, dripping with water. He had a towel around him that made him look more like a sweating sumo wrestler than a clean and refreshed man. He gently slapped the boy on the cheek and went by him to get dressed, "Celebrate, that's what we'll do."

"Yeah, after our meeting we can go to an amusement park. Or we could go to Burger King!" Guillermo said, giving the boy his choice, but Lucho answered instead:

"I say we go out to a bar and get some beers. Now that's the way to celebrate!"

"Did I ask you, dimwit?"

"An amusement park, now that would be fun!" Juanito answered, after a little thought.

"Great choice. Now get some nice clothes on, the both of you." Guillermo commanded looking into Lucho's eyes, partially hidden by his full cheeks and fluffy eyebrows.

"Nice clothes, for what? We're going to a bar … across the street! You know what? Okay. I'll do what you want. I always do what *you* want!" he struggled into a pair of dark green dress pants and continued his fit, "We make thousands of dollars on each trip, and where do we stay? At the worst hotel in town! We might as well be staying at a farm! What are you saving for, retirement? We've done twelve trips already, and I am absolutely sick of it. You sweat like a pig and the movies are always the same ones!" Lucho buttoned up his bright red shirt, and Juanito chuckled as the underarms on the shirt began to darken as soon as they touched his skin.

"It's called long-term planning. I think you will be in for a pleasant surprise."

"In a few minutes two men will come here and offer us a deal," Guillermo began as he took his light jacket off and fanned his shirt in the humid night air, "The son of a big drug trafficker will show up with his bodyguard and tell us what they need for this to work." He pointed his finger at Lucho and strictly instructed him, "I don't want you saying a word. You either, Juanito. If your comments relate to business, then keep them to yourself.

You can speak about other things, but don't interrupt." Lucho leaned back in his chair and looked at the ceiling, rocking his head back and forth as he made one of his regular remarks:

"Yes, master and commander...we are your *humble* slaves." He sat upright again and bowed his head with his hands together in sarcastic reverence. The man in charge pointed his thin finger at the fat glob and blew fire out of his eyes without saying a word.

"You know, I am kind of hungry, can we get some supper here?" Juanito said softly once at the bar.

"Sure thing, bud," the friendlier man assured. He pulled away from the round fold-up metal table and started toward the counter without taking his eyes off of Lucho, who had his arms lazily folded over his belly.

A black SUV pulled up as a young woman took Guillermo's order. It was a Dodge Durango, and it shone like a million stars as the street lights flashed off of the carefully waxed body of the car.

"Give me a steak for the boy, and a *Coca-Cola*," Guillermo's voice was tensing up and he kept turning his head around to look at the compelling view of the four-by-four. "A few *Paceñas* also... please."

"No prol'm sir. It'll be right over," the young waitress answered, smacking her red lips as she flung her hair from one shoulder to the other.

A tall, well-built black man from the Yungas got out of the driver's seat and strode effortlessly around the front of the car without showing any emotion at all. He opened the passenger door and a young *Camba* stepped out wearing dark sunglasses and a light blue silk shirt unbuttoned halfway down his chest to reveal a golden cross on a chain and a thousand curly black hairs. Guillermo grabbed another fold-up table and set it next to the one already in use.

"Good evening, sir," Guillermo said, extending his hand to the young man. The newcomer ignored the hand as he pulled his sunglasses off to look at the interior of the trashy bar. After a few seconds he grabbed the thin man's hand and shook it vigorously, giving him a friendly slap on the shoulder as he whispered:

"Good spot. But this had better be quick and to the point. Don't even think about messing with me." He took a seat in the chair facing the wall and took out a cigarette, as his bodyguard leaned down and intended to light it, "Sit down. You're acting like a fool, *Lobo*."

"My name's Guillermo Salvatierra, he's Lucho, and…" The thin man was sharply cut off by the young man:

"Why is there a boy here? This is strictly a business meeting." He licked his lips and stared Juanito down as the boy looked at the floor.

"He works for me as well…" Guillermo replied but was quickly shut up by the other man's retort:

"In my line of work we don't deal with children. I leave that to the kidnapper's and child abusers, you understand me?" He said, blowing a puff of smoke across the table into Guillermo's face.

"He was our guinea pig during our trips to Paraguay by bus. He sat ahead of us with the merchandise and if he got caught, the person next to him would be held responsible, as simple as that." Guillermo explained, trying to stay calm and convincing. Another puff of smoke followed the silence as the young man finally continued:

"Well I guess your little boy is out of a job." A parade of thoughts ran through Juanito's mind as he thought about what that would mean.

"No, please," Guillermo protested, "You don't even have to pay him. I'm taking care of him for his father who is in prison. He's a good boy and he's helpful, he won't ever…"

"This is a bunch of bull, and you know it. I come here to do business and you land me in this." The young man dumped the ashes of his cigarette on the floor and shook his head in frustration. "Okay. Let's get this done; I'm almost out of time." He rolled the sleeve up on his shirt and rattled his golden watch around his wrist until he could see the time. "Look. My name is Jonás Gutierrez, and this is my assistant, Lobo." Lobo grew restless in the small chair and kept signaling with his eyes that is was time to go. "It will cost you somewhere in the neighborhood of ten thousand dollars." Lucho gulped hard and his black eyes stared at the table. "But you should make at least four times that much in the end. I will lend you one of my trucks and protection. Lobo and I will go in the first car, and your driver, which I suppose is Lucho, will take the truck accompanied by one of my men." He motioned at the fat man with his eyes and Lucho nodded in response to the supposition.

"No problem. We got that kind of money. Give me the address to pick up the merchandise and the date we leave." Guillermo said, sprawling his legs out and leaning back in his chair as the waiter began to come to their table.

"Here," Jonás said, sliding a folded paper over to the thin man.

"Who are the beers for?" the young waitress said putting one hand on her hip and the other under the platter she held by her head. She looked to be about eighteen or nineteen and her glistening black eyes showed her shallowness.

"Beer for me and my partner," Lucho said, indicating the other one to go over to Guillermo, "Give the boy the pop and the plate."

"How about you boys, a few beers, a coke, how about…" Guillermo said after a long swig of his cold beer.

"No, we were just leaving. I can't be drunk at my father's wedding." He smiled and got up, motioning Lobo to turn the car on.

"Really, isn't he a little old for that?" The fat man said, emphasizing it with a disgusting burp.

"Yeah, he's almost as old as God; but when you're rich, it's deep pockets that count—not a deep heart." Jonás got up from his chair and buttoned up a couple of buttons on his silk shirt as a mild breeze flew through the large doors of the bar. "Fell in love with this *gringa* from Switzerland. She's a little younger than me." He gave a wink as he shook hands, first with Guillermo, then with Lucho, and lastly he gave a pat on Juanito's head.

"Thanks, *compadre*!" Lucho yelled as the rich man got into his truck and took off. "Say, what day are we taking off?" He asked, now looking at Guillermo.

"Let's see," Guillermo says, scanning the paper Jonás gave him, "Friday—that's in two days in case you couldn't count." The thin man answered, giving a loud laugh. His thin frame was already feeling the effect of the beer after the first bottle. Lucho had to go the bathroom twice before he ever felt the effect of the brew.

"You should join a circus. Excuse me; I have to go to the bathroom." Lucho nudged Juanito and continued: "Don't let him do anything; he's a complete idiot when he's drunk."

"S're," Juanito said indistinctly, as he continued gnawing on the thick ball of steak in his mouth. He chewed and chewed until he finally gave up and spit it into a napkin. Some people, like Lucho, seemed to have been born into Middle School, and they never leave.

"You know Juan. We're gonna be... *big*. Real big! We're gonna be som'tin in life. Not like that lard over there!" Guillermo slouched farther back in his seat and called out to the waitress, "Girl! Another beer, now!"

"Yeah, I know what you mean. Lucho is just too big." Juanito commented as he ate some greasy rice.

"You got that son. I'll give you some more advice. You see that girl over there..." Guillermo went on to give a long discourse in his drunken state.

In the bathroom of the bar Lucho pulled out his cellphone and made a call. His voice was hushed and low. "Hey Andres, this is Lucho. Round up your boys, I got a big job on Friday. *Friday*, you hear?" he paused and listened intently and then continued, now in a louder tone, "I'll call you back tomorrow when I have some more time to explain the ordeal. Be there, or I'll have you for supper!" he hung up without waiting for a response and went back into the bar and ordered a few more beers for his table. The bar slowly filled up with sweaty bodies and loud music blasted away, sending its sound to everybody within a mile radius. Not exactly the party Juanito was expecting!

Chapter Ten

It was one of the many blistering days that the thermometer broke the century mark in Santa Cruz, with the humidity not relenting at all in the stale air. People's faces were hanging lower than usual and their backs were covered in sweat—even thought it was just ten in the morning. The sun was like a hot flame warming up an oven. Just a few clouds were visible, but more were rapidly forming. They say man has no instinct, but we have acquired knowledge, and we can sometimes guess as to the future with good accuracy. Today was like that, even though the *celeste* sky was barely covered, everyone knew they would have a very heavy downpour, mixed with the barbaric clashes of an electric storm.

"Get off of me!" the large man growled, shaking his

arms vigorously to move the guards away. He was handcuffed, and wasn't wearing a shirt, showing his floppy belly, covered by a thick carpet of salt and pepper hair. The guards held the man with their iron arms as they sat him down on a chair opposite a boy. "What am I going to do—escape? Ha! I'm leaving in a few months, why would I escape!" He shook his head in disgust and reached up with both hands and fixed his hair as he looked over at the boy: "Hey bud! Why didn't you come and visit me last week?" Juanito shifted in his seat uncomfortably as he looked over at his demanding father.

"One of our trips, you know. We took more than a week this time, sorry. Guillermo…" he paused, slapping his neck violently, as a mosquito slipped away.

"Whatever, just as long as you give me my money—and a lot of it—I'll be fine. Cigarettes keep going up, not to mention…" The sweaty man jerked his right arm behind him and slapped a mosquito himself, leaving a small pool of his own blood on his hand. "Man, I cannot wait to get out of this *dump*!" he yelled as he slapped at his back and arm a couple more times. Juanito pulled a package out of his old backpack and slid it through the entrance to his father's soft hands.

"Calm down," one of the guards cautioned, "Talk at a normal level, and no…"

"Why can't I speak to my child in my apartment? We could sit beside the air conditioner and not have to worry about these absurd bugs!" Juanito's father raged as he put the package of money in his pocket. He then bribed the officers, "What do you want—two hundred or three?" He pulled some red bills out of his pocket and offered them to the officers. One officer reached out to accept the money, but the other one hit the prisoner's hands down and then raised him up to his feet by his underarms.

"We don't do favors for anyone. Do we, officer?" He looked his assistant square in the eyes.

"Of course not, I was just going to ... " the other guard said, attempting to cover it up, when the other guard cut him off in disgust.

"Let's go prisoner. We'll escort you to your room." He violently pulled the large man to his feet he began to lead him out the door.

"You have an air conditioner?" Juanito asked in disbelief, getting up and speaking loudly through the opening in the glass wall.

"Of course, I have cable TV, internet, a double bed, and much more. If these idiots would let you in, maybe we could have a *civilized* conversation!" By the time he said the last words, he was yelling as he got farther and farther away from his son. The door was shut and the boy began walking out of the room he had been in so many times. He got up and walked to the door. He had forgotten to tell his dad that he loved him. He shrugged his shoulders and walked out the door. His dad would've thought it silly anyway, like the other times.

"Thank you, sir. Could you let me out?" Juanito asked a guard outside, and he led him to the front gate and let him out of the Palma Sola Prison.

This was just a repetition of what had happened so many times. He'd walk in, give his father the money, and then make his way back onto the street. He would get on a bus and head home with just a few meager pesos left over from the money he had given his father.

It was the day before Guillermo, Lucho, and Juanito would take off with the truck owner, so the guys spent all day getting prepared for the trip, picking up the merchandise, buying supplies—all in the excruciating heat of the city. The entire day went by without anyone remembering their promise to the boy. His birthday came and went, and sadness filled everything Juanito did. Guillermo asked him a couple of times what was going on, but the boy did not answer, hoping someone would remember. But no one did. That night, at about ten o'clock, back at the hotel, Guillermo and Lucho were discussing their trip anxiously on the bed, as the television blasted a rap video. Juanito, on the other hand, sat on the balcony, with the door closed and watched as the sky began to fall.

   The entire sky was black, not a single star to be seen. Heavy clouds began unleashing their day's work onto the hot earth, and you could see steam coming off the ground as the first drops fell. A strange music filled the earth as the rain began to rip through the atmosphere and fall with its full force on the pavement, tin roofs, car hoods, and long grass. It was a symphony—letting off disorderly, yet rhythmic music for the ears of the Conductor. Juanito sat on a low stool and looked out as the blankets of rain began crashing upon the city. You could hear swearing from Lucho as the cable was disconnected at the central station for fear of damage. And it was good that they unplugged their satellites when they did, for the *best* was yet to come.

   Bright lights began breaking through the thick ceiling of the sky as lightning flashed silently into the earth and was followed, seconds later, by the heart-wrenching blast of thunder that ripped through the aerospace. And these overwhelming sounds were followed with rushing wind that threw warm droplets onto Juanito's face. The birthday boy's face lit up white, his eyes twinkled, and a look of awe followed as he wiped the water from his face.

Angels playing baseball is how I explain this beautiful catastrophe. Silence fills the sky, as athletic angels hit the ball as far as they can, all eyes following the strike. It is only when the ball hits the earth that the crowd goes into an uproar—and what a crowd it is!

Chapter Eleven

Dreams are the rope
That hold a broken man together.
Hope keeps a man
From becoming a maniac,
From despairing and dying.
When all that is worth keeping,
Has been lost,
Our soul tells us to fight on,
To break barriers and
Close our eyes:
To see the colors of the future,
To taste the beauty of tomorrow.
For all men have been broken,
But only the ones who persevere
Live their dreams.

The next day brought a beautiful afternoon, with clouds hovering in the air all over the city of Santa Cruz; it was cool and fresh, unlike many days that are oppressively hot and muggy. The city was festive in preparation for Christmas—a tropical Christmas. Juanito looked out of the window of the red Ford 250 at all the people, busily shopping for presents. Thousands of people flocked the open market on one of the main avenues, making traffic desperately slow.

According to law, city buses are entitled to the far right lane, leaving two open lanes for lighter traffic. But this law is rarely followed, even though Policemen regularly try and direct the busy streets during rush hours, they cannot stop the disorder. For about a hundred meters before they reach the handful of policemen, all the old buses line up on the right. But the very second they pass the law, they put the pedal to the metal on their slow, diesel engines, and roar past smaller vehicles, into their lanes, leaving behind a toxic bed of smog and drops of old oil on orderly and civilized cars in the next two lanes.

One has to be fast in Santa Cruz—quick as lightning on the shift, a hot puncher on the pedal, and own a junkyard car to even dare and threaten these metal-eating road-hogs. Guillermo, who was at the wheel, wouldn't dare try, even though the huge truck he drove was stronger and faster than the buses. He stayed far on the left, keeping as close as possible to the car ahead of him to not get cut off. It was not his truck he was driving, it was Jonás'. The young owner of this vehicle was a few stop signs ahead of Guillermo and Juanito. Lucho was in the truck with one of the young rich man's workers. They were waiting up ahead for orders.

"Lucho. Lucho. Do you copy? Over." The rash voice of Jonás on the radio filled the small cab of Guillermo's car.

"I copy. Over." Another voice came over now, heavier and deeper, it was obviously the man in the truck with Lucho.

"You're free to go now. I'm past your spot on the fourth ring," the first voice crackled through the speaker, then Jonás took a breath and continued in a louder voice, "Give him some room, Guillermo. Keep your radio on at all times and make sure the volume is high. Over."

"Sure thing…Uh…Over." Guillermo replied, slightly turning up the volume on the radio that was attached to the roof of the pickup. Juanito continued staring out of his window at the crowds of people. They were almost out of the jam and Guillermo noticed the anxiety in the boy, so he spoke up, kindly, "You know we'll be back for Christmas. We'll go shopping for something for you. What do you think you'd like?" The thin man kept his eyes peeled to the road, but every once in awhile he peeked over to look at the boy.

"Oh. I don't know. I would like one of those remote control cars," the boy's eyes lit up as he looked ahead, silently dreaming. But then he looked at the turned face of Guillermo, and not seeing a response, he spoke to the red sports shirt he had on: "You don't have to get me anything, don't worry."

"Funny boy. I'm not getting you a remote control car. I'll get you a remote control helicopter. Better yet, I'll buy you a Playstation 3! I saw them being sold downtown."

"Really? But…we don't have a television." Juanito said, his excitement quickly running out.

"I'm gonna buy a huge plasma TV, a few couches, a large bed, and a house to put it all in." Guillermo said, with a wide grin on his face.

"Yeah right!" Juanito laughed and pushed air out of his loosely closed lips, spitting saliva over the floor, imitating the sound of one of the diesel buses that had just cut them off at full speed.

"I haven't told Lucho yet, but I'm out of this business as of this trip. I'm gonna leave him to make up his own team. With the profit I get out of this sale I'll start my own business."

"Will I stay with Lucho then?" Juanito asked, worried.

"No, of course not. Not unless you want to live with that lard!" Guillermo said, looking straight at the boy.

"No!"

"Well, you can stay with me until your dad is out of prison. How does that sound?"

"Awesome!" the young boy said, a relieved smile falling on his brown face.

The caravan was taking an isolated road to Paraguay, to escape the Government Patrols. These secondary dirt roads were over fifty years old, but still in excellent condition from little use. They were built and connected in huge grids that crisscrossed at right angles every few miles. So the roads were perfectly straight, with long stretches of absolutely nothing for miles. The caravan had driven through the night and as the morning sun rose over the horizon, they grew increasingly tired.

It is on one of these long deserted stretches that we

will stop and look on. The lightly packed red dirt moves slowly over the flat road with the breeze. For miles on end you may not ever see any cattle, houses, farms, and definitely no water. But do not be mistaken, people do live out here—like in the Wild West of old, with their own rules and laws. Most of them raise cattle, and they dig ponds to hold rain water to keep them alive. Some *haciendas* own thousands of heads of cattle, but they keep them well concealed in their enormous blocks of land.

"Can you give me some more *tereré*? I'm dying of thirst here," Lobo said, as he lay back in the comfortable seat of the car and drove down the lonely stretch of land, with the air conditioner blasting out all the cold it could muster without overheating the engine.

"Sure thing." Jonás said, getting the thermos of cold water and pouring it into the gourd.

The Dodge Durango speeds past the place where we are stationed at close to fifty miles an hour and a huge cloud of dust covers us as he passes. The dust eventually settles, and you can just barely see the black four by four disappearing in the distance.

Suddenly, two men run out of the tangled bushes carrying a long pipe.

"Hurry up. He'll be here any second," one man yelled to the other. They both ran back into the thicket and came out hurriedly, each carrying a different item as they began assembling a blockade. A metal pole was hoisted onto two pillars at either side of the road and a six foot tall box, painted white and yellow was set next to the right end of it.

"I am so tired of *traveling*." The sound erupted from the radio attached to the belt of one of the men.

"That's the signal. Get in the box and I'll be across the road in the bushes," the man yelled as he hustled into the thorn trees with his rifle and quietly waited. The sun was just rising and a red sun filled the horizon at the end of the road. Silence filled the air as a big Volvo truck began plowing down the road a ways away; the sound of the engine slowly getting louder and louder. The man in the box closed his eyes quickly and recited a prayer, sweat pouring down his face.

"What's this, a patrol … what about Jonás? He didn't even warn us! Something is going on …" The man sitting next to Lucho exclaimed. He quickly picked up the radio.

"Keep cool!" Lucho calmly said, taking the radio out of the other man's hand and slowing the truck down, "We can get out of this, just act calm. I want you to get down and talk to the guard and bribe him to let us through." Lucho shifted down and drove at a crawl as he approached the stop, "Remember, just stay calm and he will treat you better … Go!"

"Okay. You're right, I'll just …" His voice faded as he got out of the tall truck cab and closed the door. He walked up to the guard and began talking to him. Lucho held up his hand and winked at the guard. He nodded.

"Jonás, you copy? Jonás?" Lucho said into the microphone of the radio.

"What's up? Over," came the reply.

"We got a flat tire. Hurry up about it! Over."

"We'll be there in a couple of minutes. Over," Jonás replied calmly.

Lucho then gave thumbs up to the guard just as his helper turned around.

Poof! The sound of a .22 rang out its sharp blast. It threw the confused helper to the ground a couple of feet away.

"Throw him into the thicket and get ready for the next two cars," Lucho commanded, as he stepped out of the drivers' seat of the truck and jumped to the ground, dust flying all around him as he landed. "And get rid of the fake stop." The two men struggled to move the helper's body across the road, since he was still not dead. He struggled to shake free and blubbered as blood spilled out of his mouth. "Quickly!" the large body of Lucho jogged over to the body, leaned over and rolled the body into the thicket.

"I'm going to get sick." One of the men grabbed his mouth and made convulsive noises as he leaned over.

"Get sick later, not now. We still have four people to kill... sissy." Lucho barked at the man with distaste. The men quickly dismantled the false Government Patrol and threw the pieces into the brush.

"Every time we do these trips it just gives me a sickening feeling," Guillermo said, glancing over at Juanito. They were a just a couple of miles behind the truck and the thin man wondered what the problem was up ahead and anxiety filled him, "We could get caught by the Police, or assaulted, anything could happen. It just scares me to do this job, that's why this is my last trip."

"What scares you about it?" Juanito asked, as he slumped back into his seat listening to the CD playing softly in the player.

"I don't know. Just the gut feeling of knowing I'm doing wrong," he sighed and took a long sip of water before continuing in a more pensive tone now, "Once I get done here I'm going to get right. Get right with God."

"Will you go and see Ana?" the boy innocently asked, but Guillermo just laughed,

"She'd slap me!" He laughed some more thinking of such an occasion, "I guess I could try... except she is probably married already and has a couple of children."

"So by getting right with God, does it mean we have to go to the cathedral and listen to some boring priest talking in that odd language?" Another laugh erupted from Guillermo as he shook his head,

"No. We're going to go to an Evangelical church," Guillermo said, grabbing his bottle of warm water and drinking some more, an action he had repeated thousands of times during the long, dehydrating trip.

"There's the truck!" Juanito said; he pointing down the road at the truck parked in the middle of the road.

"I'll get out and check on him, you can come with me if you want."

"I think I'll stay in here," the boy decided.

"Okay then, I'll leave the engine on and the A/C running." Guillermo stopped the large four by four a few meters behind the truck and got down. "Which tire is flat, Lucho?" Guillermo asked in a loud voice, stooping behind the truck to look at the duellies in back. Just as he ducked the sound of a rifle went off, and a bullet whizzed near his balding head.

"Hey Guillermo!" the sarcastic voice of Lucho came from the front of the truck. Guillermo quickly backed up and hit the bumper of the Ford. His eyes darted, looking for any movement. He looked into the thicket and was surprised to see the body of a man there, dead and bleeding in a heap. A man was also there, quickly reloading his gun. "There is a new boss in town," Lucho growled, his voice now nearer.

Juanito got into a crouched position after hearing the shot, shaking with fear. He took a quick glance up and Guillermo signaled that the boy get down as he struggled to get the door open. A bullet burned the air and hit him in the left arm, the impact making Guillermo want to faint. But he kept his head and opened the door, flinging his body into the car, keeping as low as possible.

"Stay down, bud," he said, shaking like a leaf in a hard wind. "We're gonna... gonna get out of here." He shifted into first gear and punched the accelerator, the tires spinning out for a couple seconds. A cloud of smoke and red dirt covered the vehicle as another shot went off. The bullet hit the door frame as the car raced forward.

"What's going on?" the boy asked, as he crouched on the floor.

"Stay down!" Guillermo drove with just a few inches of his head over the dashboard. His arm began to bleed profusely, but he clamped his jaw and focused ahead. He circled the large truck, but the impulse pushed them into the ditch on the side. He skidded sideways but managed to pull the truck back onto the road. He glanced over to see the furious face of Lucho yelling at him. He pulled the trigger of his pistol and shattered the back and side window. Guillermo briefly saw Jonás' car, with him dead in the passengers' seat, bleeding from the head. He had come back because of a false flat tire and ended up being the one punctured.

"I'm scared!" the boy yelled desperately.

"I know. Hold on." The boy got up from the floor and huddled in the seat. Guillermo constantly looked out of his rear view window after he passed Lucho and his gang. They threw out the dead bodies and all got into the Durango and began the chase. Guillermo now pushed into the top gear and raced down the dusty road. His arm began pulsating as he held the wheel tightly. "Ah!" The thin man gave out a sharp yelp as he grabbed his left arm and felt the warm blood flowing out of the open wound.

"What is it?" the boy asked, "Are you hurt?"

"I'm okay. Just a little cut, bud," Guillermo said, trying to stay calm as he again retook the steering wheel, his hand dripping with the blood of his arm. The red sun blared into Guillermo's eyes, causing him to see spots. "Damn! Why would he do this now?" the man exclaimed—a million thoughts flying through his mind, in all shapes and colors.

"They are getting closer!" Juanito yelled looking through the broken back window to the Durango that was two or three-hundred meters back and gaining.

"Hang on!" The man yelled as he clutched the wheel even harder with his throbbing arms. He blinked his eyes rapidly from the pain of looking straight into the sun. Then the intersection appeared. He took his foot off the acceleration pedal and took a ninety degree turn while almost standing on the brakes. All four wheels locked and the car skidded into the wide berth around the corner. A rooster tail of sand and uprooted plants followed as the truck slammed into the thick wall of thorny trees. Guillermo quickly took his foot off of the brake and pounded the acceleration pedal as he downshifted. The car roared like lightning as it bolted forward and came out of the trees, uprooting more brushes as the car convulsed violently, clawing for traction. The small boy grabbed his knees in fear as the truck roared and shook violently. Guillermo yelled in pain but kept on going, through the maze.

That was when he hit the rock protrusion under the left wheel. That part of the car came to a complete stop. It sent the rest of the vehicle spinning around the axis. The impact sent the steering wheel out of place and it slammed into the chest cavity of Guillermo. The smell of burnt oil and brake fluid filled the cabin and Juanito coughed for air. The truck smashed into the trees after going around a half circle, sending the bruised body of the fragile boy onto the door. Guillermo's eyes were still open, still having a few more seconds of life left. His entire body was crushed, but the man did not feel the pain anymore.

"Run," he whispered to Juanito.

"I'm going to die! Help me Guillermo!" The boy looked over to the face of his friend and struggled for breath himself. Fear grasped him. The sound of the other car roaring down the road was the next thing he heard. The boy took one more look at the stone face of Guillermo before reaching for the door handle. He pushed the door to open, but it was held back by a mass of broken branches. The black Durango came around the corner at a more controlled pace and then roared past the red Ford. Juanito flung himself out of the window and landed on the thicket of thorny trees. His skin broke open as he ran forward through the more open parts of land under the trees.

Chapter Twelve

Juanito emerged from under a thorn bush and stopped, grabbed his knees and coughed for air. He stood up straight and looked about him. A tall cactus loomed over him and a couple more small thorny trees grew here and there. The boy's eyes were swollen, tired from crying and from running. After he left the truck, he ran with all of his might though the desert, wondering why all that had happened. It had all happened so quickly, without warning. The young boy crouched under a tree and leaned his sore body against its slim trunk. His shirt was torn to shreds and his jeans were hanging onto his body by mere threads that hung together longwise across his bleeding thighs. His hair looked more like a birds nest than the neatly combed black hair that usually clung to him. A huge gash under his right eye had bled down his face and stained his once-white shirt. The hot wind had dried the blood and mixed it with fine crystals of sand. His small blue backpack clung to his sweaty back, covered in dirt and thorny twigs.

"Water, water…" he whispered to himself as he scrounged through his backpack now sitting between his legs. A couple of shirts were shoved in there along with some shorts, underwear, socks, etc. He found an empty bottle of water. He opened it and a couple drops fell onto his dry tongue and disappeared into it. He set the bottle next to him and curled up as if to receive the most benefit from the meager shade the tree he was sitting under provided. Juanito strained his sore eyes as he looked around him in light of the early-morning sun. He was lost. Everything looked the same—dirt, thorns, rocks…

He noticed a strange looking rock sitting under the tree next to him and the boy stared at it with curiosity. It was grayish-brown and had an almost sharp top edge. He closed his eyes and leaned back in relaxation, but his mind was pounding. Pictures of the white cross he had seen on the road to Paraguay flashed in his head. Stories filled his mind as tears again began to flow over his reddened eyes. He knew he needed to keep going, but where to? Everything looked the same.

A distant and vaguely familiar sound filled his ears as he sat up and looked about him. His eye caught site of an animal scurrying by him into the thicket. The boy struggled to his feet and realized that that animal that had just crossed him was the rock he had seen under the other tree. It was an Iguana. He shuffled his feet forward as he put his backpack back on. He sighed and walked on in the growing heat.

Again he heard that same noise. The young boy now recognized the sound and turned his head in the direction of the noise. It was the bark of a dog. Again the sound repeated, now by more than one dog, and the boy bolted forward into the thorny mesh towards the sound. He scrambled through the trees, cutting himself in various places. Through the branches he saw a small adobe house and his eyes lit up at the sight of it. He ran as fast as he could, not taking his eyes off of the structure. As he was about to run through the last thorn tree, a broken branch caught him in his side. A trail of blood slowly spurted out of the long wound, but the boy did not take note.

A large concrete rain water reservoir, filled to the brim with fresh water, caught the boy's eye and he ran to it. Just then two black Dobermans appeared about twenty yards away, and they began barking incessantly at the boy; the only thing holding them back were the ropes around their necks. Juanito cupped water out and onto his bloody face with his filthy hands. The dogs strained their thin necks, standing up on their hind feet as the leather ropes held them back. Their mouths slobbered onto the dry earth and barked loudly, but their commotion didn't bother the thirsty boy.

Poof! The sound of a large rifle filled the air, as a bullet thundered close to the boy's head. The dogs backed away, whimpering, as an empty bronze cartridge glided out of the gun and jingled on the floor. Two dusty leather boots stomped onto the wooden planks, making them creak. Wrinkled gray pants, red lining their outside edge, were stuffed into the boots. An old gray suit jacket with silver bands on its shoulders and a short cross and an eagle on its chest sat on the slumped body of a very old man. The lasting pieces of growing white hair on his scalp were overgrown in certain places to shadow the increasing baldness. His dark blue eyes lined up the end of his gun with the boy across the patio, and his fingers twitched on the trigger.

"Vhat ar' you doing here?" the old man's grungy voice yelled across the patio.

"I..." the boy ducked behind the cement tank and swallowed hard. Another shot raced a few feet over the boy's head. In terror Juanito grabbed his knees and shook.

"Otto, Otto! Vhat is it?" The voice of another man was heard now. It was not as harsh as the other man's had been, but it was deeper and held more authority.

"Ther' is a wild boy back ther'!" The other man answered. The old man loaded his gun again and cocked it as hundreds of metal dust particles fell to the floor due to the rusty old rifle's oxidation. But as he aimed, the other man reached over and pulled the gun down.

"Put it down, Otto. Take a seat over there," Otto slowly handed his gun over and went to take a seat, as he held his lower back in pain, his bony hands shaking as he grabbed for the armrests of the chair and took a seat. The other man slowly moved down the steps of the front of the house and began to go towards the reservoir. Juanito carefully peered around the corner of his refuge and was shocked at the sight. A tall man, just over six feet, strode slowly at the boy. He was only a little younger than the other man, but he looked stronger and healthier. He was not dressed as an army officer; instead he had on a pair of jeans and a white shirt. His hair was gray as well, but not balding as much as the other man. But that was not what was shocking. His face, shirt, and part of his pants were covered in blood. The blood dripped from his arms and whiskered chin as the man walked forward.

"I didn't mean...any harm, sir...I..." Juanito stumbled over his words as he crawled away from the reservoir.

"It's okay. vhat's your name, son?" The old man wiped his chin and splattered blood onto the ground. He cleaned his hands on the back of his jeans and outstretched a hand to the frightened boy.

"Juan...Juan..." the boy reached for the hand slowly and let himself be helped up as he stuttered.

"Great. My name's Hans." He looked over at his friend sitting in a chair in the shade of the tin roof and nodded.

"Well, my name is actually..." the boy was now on his feet and he dusted his clothes clean as he tried to explain but was cut off:

"This is just a boy, Otto! Vy vere you shooting at him, eh?" Hans said as he dipped a small metal basin into the water and began washing blood off of his arms.

"Vell, if he's a Jew, I'll know soon enough," Otto responded as he struggled to get out of his seat.

"Sit down," Hans told him as he walked by the skinny old man. Otto was now standing up and was fixing an odd hat onto his head that had a distinct line of white and red from where it had given him shade. "How many times do I have to tell you—there are no Jews in Bolivia."

"Bolibia? Vhere is that? Ve ar' in Germany, the Empire that vill last a thousand years!" he argued, almost yelling now.

"Sit down, Otto. Get some rest." Hans said as he went around the side of the adobe house. He yelled back to the boy as he kept on walking, "Boy, drink some vater, clean up, and then come behind the house and help me."

"Soldiers do not sleep," Otto yelled still more, as he slowly took his seat, "Hans, you make me sick! You are not a soldier, but a veakling. Ve must conquer, for as the Third Reich himself said, 'Conquest is not a right, but a duty.'" The old man reached onto a table next to him, picked up a book, and began to read. Juan carefully looked at it and couldn't decipher the strange letters that read *Mein Kampf*. The boy quietly drank water out of the reservoir until he was full. He washed his face and arms clean and changed his shirt. Juan quietly walked by the old man reading the book. The man eyed the boy carefully up and down. His eyes seemed to fill with fire when the boy looked at him. Juan quickened his pace to go around the house but he heard the old man whisper, "Jew."

The rest of the morning was filled with hard work and little talking. Juan was shocked to see some things he had never seen his whole life. As he went behind the small adobe house he saw a large dead boar. Hans had punctured its heart, and pools of blood sat below the wild boar's hairy body. The old man explained that the best way to kill any kind of animal is by hitting it straight in the heart, but it is also the hardest way to kill them. Hans had expertly pierced the heart of the bore and, in consequence, blood flew out of the open organ onto anything in its way, including the old man.

Juan looked on for what seemed an eternity as the old man carefully stripped the skin off of the warm body of the bore, using a sharp blade to cut the fat lying between the meat and the thick leathery skin. The young boy spent most of the morning running to get water when Hans needed it. All that morning Otto sat in his rocking chair, snoring loudly as he slept.

Juan threw up in the bushes as Hans inserted a sharp knife into the chest cavity of the pig, ripping through the meat from just below the neck until the other extremity. 'Vater, vater!' were the words Juan heard over and over as he ran to fetch water. Hans' flabby arms became lost between the internal organs of the pig as he snipped out the desired pieces. Hans gave the most attention at pulling out the large intestine, carefully pulling out about twenty feet of it. Most of the other organs he threw at his dogs so they could eat it. But he made an exception for the heart, which Hans said was the most delicious piece of meat in all animals.

As the mid-morning sun began threatening, Hans whistled loudly, giving a distinctive call. A few minutes later, Otto hobbled around the edge of the house and appeared. To Juan's surprise, the old man shook the young boy's hand heartily as if it were the first time they had met. Hans and the boy waited around as Otto changed from his German officers' suit into more suitable clothes. Then all three of them struggled to carry the carcass of the wild boar into the shade. There they split into two groups. Otto began cutting the thicker pieces of meat into small cubes. After that he began cutting the rest of the meat into long, thin pieces, hanging them on long wires running from a tree to the side of the house. Hans and Juan began cleaning the small intestine. In half an hour they turned a sticky and clogged piece of intestine into what looked more like a very skinny and long piece of a plastic bag. Then the final procedure began:

The small cubes of meat were fed into a meat grinder. All three of them took turns turning the handle slowly, while the other held the intestine in place and fed the ground meat carefully into it. The third person, usually Juan, sprinkled various spices into the top of the meat grinder. Juan asked what the spices were, and the old men tried to explain what they were, but without luck, repeating German words over and over without saying anything understandable to the boy's ears.

As the noonday sun rose, everyone was covered in sweat, but it was a morning well-used. They had made sausage and they had several kilos of meat drying on the wires. For lunch Otto fried up the heart in a heavy frying pan on an open fire. Hans boiled some yucca as Juan looked on, not knowing how to help.

The afternoon was spent in relaxation. Both men took a long naps that lasted from around noon until four or five. Juan spent the day getting to know the dogs and climbing some of the bigger trees in the area. When his new acquaintances got up, they began making supper—boar meat; so Juan was given the job of taking all of the meat off wires as the sun began to go down late in the summer day. And soon after that it was off to bed. Before seven had come, all of them were sound asleep.

Hans and the boy slept inside the adobe hut, while Otto got the privilege of sleeping outside on the hammock. It had been an odd day—a strange, yet natural introduction to the Chaco.

Chapter
Thirteen

Darkness was the first sign of the long day, as Juan got the urge to go to the bathroom. He climbed off the hard, cornhusk-filled mattress and quietly walked out the open door into the cool night air. The boy stepped carefully on the dark ground in the light of the sky to avoid any kind of sharp object that might hurt his feet. Once he thought he had gone far enough away he went to the bathroom. He looked up and was suddenly amazed by a very different sky than what the city of Santa Cruz, his past home, usually offered. Millions upon millions of stars seemed to stare at the boy in the quiet of the night. And once Juan had zipped up his battered pants he kept looking up as he turned and gazed in amazement at the silver moon, letting his mouth drop open in awe. It glowed so brightly it hurt the boy's eyes. The sphere looked so close; one could almost reach out and touch the enormous object that seemed to float in the sky like a large silver coin.

The pensive silence was cut short by the sound of metal grinding against another piece of metal. The young boy tiptoed behind the side of the adobe hut. He slowly went around the left side of it, looking around curiously until the sound suddenly stopped. A sharp yell followed, and then a silence, followed shortly after by the same grinding metal sound. Juan spotted where the noise came from and watched silently in the shadow of the house. He looked on as a sleek, black gun was assembled. It looked like a specialized machine gun, and its body shone in the moonlight. Clever hands had assembled the pieces of this submachine gun in record time. It was Otto. His gray hair was covered by a small black hat, and he was again wearing his uniform. The old man put the gun on his shoulder as he let out a short yell. He raised his other arm straight out at about fifty-five degrees and again let out another yell. Juan remained quiet in the shadows with his eyebrows raised in curiosity.

Otto put his arm down, then his gun, setting it carefully on a table in front of him. He robotically turned on his right foot, away from Juan and walked toward a large picture that was hung on the only wall of the open shed. About twenty feet separated Juan from the old man now; so the boy half-crawled, half-ran, across the opening, and hid behind a large crate to watch the strange old man. Again the old man lifted his arm straight and pointed at the picture and yelled:

"Heil, Hitler!"

The boy moved his feet behind him slowly in order to get a closer look through the small space between the crate and a pole. The old man got down onto his knees with a youthful spirit, but his body ached as it creaked on its hinges to get into the position his memory asked for. Otto grabbed the black book from off a small table and began reciting words in German as he held his hand up to the small black book.

A small noise surprised both the boy and the old man, and as quick as lightning the old man was off and looking around for the place the sound had come from. It had probably been some small animal, but the old man was not persuaded. So as the old man approached, Juan carefully moved around the crate to keep out of his view. Luckily, he succeded to keep hidden and the hobbled old soldier ran off around the house and dissappeared into some trees. Juan wanted to see what Otto had been doing, but he dared not to, so in his fear he ran off to the front porch, and crept into the house. He breathed hard in the cool night air as he sat on his cot and Hans momentarily tossed and turned in his bed, but eventually went back to his dream. And soon enough Juan would join him, going into a strange and blood-bathed dream.

When Juan awoke early the next morning he immediately remembered what had happened at midnight. He slipped out of bed and went looking for Hans. As he exited the door he found Otto still sleeping, as he had hoped. Hans was in the shed, drinking a cup of steaming hot coffee from a large tin cup.

"How did you sleep last night, little man?" the man asked in between sips.

"Just fine..." the boy sat down near the place he had seen Otto the night before and rubbed his eyes as he tried to make sense of the occasion, "Actually, um... Have you ever seen Otto out... say, at night?" The boy asked slowly, choosing his words carefully, as he turned his head to make sure he wasn't being overheard. A loud laugh from Hans seemed to shake the air, as he breathed hard and continued laughing and shaking his shoulders. Juan relaxed slightly and looked down on his dirty brown feet.

"Otto... my friend Otto..." he laughed a bit more and continued on, "Yeah he make me laugh sometime, I really should've told you earlier about him. He's lost a few marbles—I think you'd understand me if I told you that."

"So he's sick?" the boy asked.

"I guess so. He isn't vell, that's vhat I do know." He took a few more sips and calmed down a bit more, "He's lost his memory. Thinks vere still in the var. Oh, Otto!"

"What war? In Bolivia?" Juan asked intently.

"No, no. In Germany, vhere ve come from. Vhen the var looked to be lost ve came over to Bolivia. Otto still thinks ve von though..."

But again the boy interrupted the man's story, "Where's Germany?"

"A long vays avay, bud. If you keep askin' me different questions, I'll never answer the first question you ask!" Hans exclaimed, shaking his head in frustration.

"I'm sorry," Juan said, kicking his heels against the wobbly chair he was sitting on.

"You're okay. Ve came here as the var became despairing for our side, as I said, and took a ship to Bolivia because ve didn't vant to go to military detention camps, so ve…" Hans clicked his fingers together and quickly explained, "Any German soldier, or any soldier in the var for that matter, vas put in a sort of prison when they vere caught by their enemy. A place I didn't want to end my life in."

"Sort of like tag then—like freeze tag?" the boy asked in innocence.

"I don't know vhat that is, but if it helps you understand vhat I am saying, okay."

"So you guys came to Bolivia…" Hans caught the slack and continued his story:

"Right, so ve came here to live. And ve've lived here for about sixty years—vow, has been long?" Hans nodded his head slowly in realization as he sipped his thick black coffee, "I guess yes since ve left Germany in the forty's vhen ve vere only teenagers and now it's…"

"So why does Otto still think you are in the war?"

"Oh, of course, I'm sorry. He's lost his memory—he easily forgets things and sometimes thinks he is still young and that ve are in the var," the old man threw the grains of his coffee onto the ground behind the boy and right away their dog came up and sniffed the area, looking for something to eat.

"So what was he yelling last night?"

"He's made up his own ritual to remind him of Hitler, the hero of the German people of that time." He shook his head in amuzement and laughed, "He believe ve von the var;" he let out a strong laugh, "poor old geezer."

"Vhat ar' you fellas' visperin' about?" Otto's grumpy

voice sounded like a big drum, with the heavy accent of someone who is still dreaming.

"Nothing very important, just telling our guest about our place…" Hans said casually.

"Who is that boy? I vould swear he's a Jew, come over here and let me look at you boy…" Otto inquired, walking up to Juan, but the sturdy arm of Hans stopped him.

"Calm down Otto, he's my friend…" He winked out of his eye at Juan who again retook his seat after a short scare.

"Vhat?" Otto asked.

"My frie-end!" he almost yelled back.

After Otto calmed down, the gang began getting ready for a trip to a neighbor's hacienda, or farmhouse, an hour away.

They split the sausage into two parts and filled two bags with it. A lively mule carried the supplies on his back as they made for the hacienda of Don Pancho. They also took three guns with them, and to Juan's surprise he was given one to carry as well. Otto became more and more amiable throughout the short trip, and soon he was in full conversation with Juan.

"No!" Otto said grabbing the gun out of Juan's hand. It shocked the boy, but it was not the crabby old man's intention to startle him. "You never ever face the barrel of a gun down. It is very dangerous, it makes it easy to pull trigger and then '*poof!*' there goes your foot."

"Like this?" Juan said, holding the gun straight across his chest. But again Otto reacted in frustration.

"*Scheisse!*" he pulled the gun out of Juan's hand and put it over the boy's back. "Put gun on your back or pointing upvard on your chest. Very simple." He took a deep breath and slowed his pace up a little, "Oh, the vorld is filled with idiots!"

"Let's take a breather Otto, let's sit down for avhile and have a drink of vater, come on." Hans waved Otto and the boy over, as he tied the mule up to a stubby tree.

"I'm sorry…" Juan said awkwardly, avoiding the old soldier's eyes.

"Don't be sorry, I vanted to help you." He grabbed the boy's shoulders with unexpected strength. Otto reached for the rifle that the boy held, and he handed it to him, but not without feeling the strain of the weight of the ancient gun in his arms. "I'll teach you how to use it. Vhat use is gun if you don't know how to use it? Even more so if you don't know how to hold it!"

The next half hour was spent with the two soldiers teaching the young boy how to shoot his gun; along with some seemingly useless information on how to line up your sights, and take apart and put together a gun.

Chapter
Fourteen

"Don Pancho...Don Pancho!" Hans called through a large wooden gate. Otto opened the gate and Hans stumbled by, leading the mule inside to begin tying him up.

A pack of dogs came racing down a long overgrown entrance, barking cheerfully to meet them. Their tails waved incessantly like flags blowing in a storm, and immediately started their passionate routine. They sniffed the two men up and down, like cops check suspects, until they got to Juan. First they looked at him carefully, then they barked menacingly, and after sensing no aggressive response, they began their scan, from toe to toe to rear end. And then they were happy.

"*Caballeros*, so glad you could come and see me. I was

getting worried about you two." He gave each a hardy hug, "I sent my boy to go and see you last week but no one was home—you are too old to be doing those tricks you know. This can't go on any longer!" He spotted Juan behind them and kneeled down to say hello, "Welcome to my humble home, my name is Ricardo Sanchez, but call me Pancho." He shook the boy's hand and ruffled his hair.

"I'm Juan Gutierrez, from Santa Cruz, and these men ... gave me a place to stay," he said shyly, rearranging his backpack by pulling the straps. It had already been a long day.

"I knew there was a heart in you Hans, a good one too. You would make a great father." Don Pancho joked.

"Vell if you find a pretty eighty year old for me, let me know and I'll be ... " Hans replied laughing a bit to himself.

"Oh, we've got the collection, I'll tell you boy, got a fine dame about ninety just behind my house," Pancho said, nodding toward the house, and the men looked puzzled, "In my family graveyard." Even Juan laughed at that.

The group joked a bit more as they walked toward the house. It was more than large. It was enormous and magnificent. It was made completely out of bright red bricks that shone beautifully in the sun's glory. Two dozen dome openings encircled the house, letting light and fresh air into the covered porch. A tall, almost pyramid of a roof covered the brick house, with an orderly covering of white roofing. Smaller houses were spotted around the main house to accommodate the workers. Many fences started at the main site and seemed to go on forever into the horizon. Beautiful citrus trees dotted the dry land, and added a special scent to the engulfing heat.

"Get us some lunch ready, Isabella," The heavy set owner half-yelled to his wife, wiping the sweat off his rippled forehead, "Let's go and have a seat in the shade, it's not a good idea to be out in the midday sun."

"Of course," Hans agreed, "Ve brought you some sausage from a boar ve skinned yesterday." He handed the owner the heavy bags and took a seat in a rocking chair.

"Splendid. You know how much I love your sausage," Pancho said as he called out for one of his workers, "Pato, give this to Isabella to stick in the freezer. And bring out a few beers." A pair of shoes clicked rapidly around the corner, and a tall, sturdy young man appeared and hurriedly took the bags to the kitchen out back.

"It's great to see you again, Pancho," Otto said, settling himself into a hammock.

"Yeah, you should definitely do the trip more often, it's not too far and we're happy to have you." Pancho unbuttoned his striped red shirt, to reveal of mat of wet hair covering his chest. He stretched out on a leather chair and let the cool air sweep over him.

"Vell," Hans responded, "Ve don't always have something to trade with you…"

"Oh, foolishness," Pancho butted in, "I'm telling you kid," he fussed, sitting up and looking straight at Juan, "These guys are real brutes—as bad as they come!" then he laughed to himself, "But I still love 'em."

"What is it that you trade?" Juan asked, getting involved in the slow-paced conversation.

"I give them a variety of things, from clothes, to guns,

to wheat and oil. You name it," Don Pancho started out, "And they bring me mostly meat and sometimes raw animal hide. Otto is also a hell of a mechanic."

"Do the animals come from your farm? Because I didn't see any livestock…" Juan asked, looking at Hans. Pancho answered and to Juan's surprise, his answer was a loud laugh, which sounded like an old car running on beer, however you interpret that.

"That's exactly why they are brutes…" Pancho explained, in between big breaths to calm down, "You give these guys a gun and a moon, and you've got something else coming your way."

"What do you mean?" the boy asked again, and Hans answered this time:

"Ve take farm animals from vell-off farmers. And ve usually do it at night." Juan nodded slowly in response, and lowered his head a bit.

"The people ve…eh…steal…from are vealthy people—they don't even realize, it's not really a problem…" Otto added, trying to explain, but it was Pancho that set them straight.

"It's all right guys—you'll always be heroes in my book, being in a war and all," he said in a calm voice, "You we're born aggressive, with strong hearts."

The group grew quiet for a while, and after some silence Isabella came and left some baked goods, a pot of hot water, and a gourd to make *poro* in. Don Pancho made up some hot tea in the cup-sized gourd and passed it to Hans as he started the conversation up again:

"Do you know who else was spirited, and I mean *spirited*?" he looked around, and not expecting an answer continued, "President Melgarejo from the 1860's."

"I learned about him in school. He was wild," Juanito added.

"Wild is a definite understatement." Pancho reached over and turned on a CD player and put on some cultural music to liven up the mood. "He was out of this world. He had a genius fit for a king, yet acted like a child most of the time in his foolishness," he chuckled a bit and continued, "I've been reading in one of my old books recently and it talked about something he did to one of his secretaries. There was this fellow who was trying very hard to get into the President's graces, and as often as he could he would come out of his office and ask the President if he could join him for a ride in his carriage. And President Melgarejo, being very busy, always said no." The *poro* was passed back to him and he filled it with some more herbs and some hot water and proceeded to pass it to Otto. "But one day he said yes."

"Thank you," Otto said softly, coughing hard afterwards.

"Anyway, the President opened the door of his carriage and let his secretary in one afternoon," Pancho continued, drawing in the attention of his guests, "He got out, closed the door and began going up on top to lead the horses. The secretary was obviously confused and asked the President why he was going to drive, and the response was a trademark, 'You said you wanted to ride with the President,'" He took a breath and continued, getting comfortable in his chair, "The president snapped at the four horses to get going and he kept on doing so until they were at full throttle pulling at the carriage, racing right through the city center. The secretary was obviously scared, wildly wondering what was happening outside the darkened carriage."

"A madman!" Otto coughed out.

"And coming to a corner, he forced the horses to turn sharply and the force sent them rolling onto the ground with the carriage behind them. But President Melgarejo, tall and athletic as always, gracefully stepped out of the carriage, and in all the public drama brushed off his fine clothes and made his way onto the sidewalk. Policemen and pedestrians came up to the President and asked him if he was okay, but he directed their attention to the secretary."

A wild roar came from Otto, who had loved the story in its entirety. Meanwhile Pato, the host's servant, came back with some beers and set them at the table. Pancho then made a poro for Juan, since he wasn't going to have a beer.

"Incredible," Hans gasped as he reached for a beer and popped it open with his back teeth.

"You know President Melgarejo pretty much lived off of beer," Pancho also reached for a beer, but opened it on a post near him. "In his drunkenness, He gave away half of Bolivia to Brazil for a white horse he had fallen in love with."

"You must be kidding," Otto sneered.

"No, it's true," Pancho assured, "In exchange for receiving the horse, he decided to have the horse put his foot on a map and wherever it landed on the Bolivian map that would go to the Brazilian President." He let that set in and finished, "When the horse's leg finally came back to the floor, the entire East part of Bolivia was covered in hoof-marks."

"I definitely missed that part in history class," Juan stated dryly.

Pancho smiled, "Of course the details about that occasion are a little jumbled, but in the end, as general history states, it came down to the drunken President wanting a certain white horse at all costs. As far as drinking goes, though, I really don't enjoy getting drunk; it makes a bad impression on others and just messes with your body." He grabbed his large gut and shook it vigorously, laughing a little.

"That's vhy you should never get drunk; it is the vorst thing that could ever happen to a man," Otto exaggerated, but with reason. He took a big gulp of his beer and used his foot to gain impulse, getting the hammock moving like a slow pendulum.

"That's for sure. Now that I remember, probably the most comical thing this President ever did was declare war on France when Napoleon Bonaparte was exiled from the country. In his drunken state he had a friend tell him in a month-old letter of the latest problems in France. And since Melgarejo, oddly, thought himself a friend of Napoleon, he woke up all his soldiers early in the morning and began to march to France." Pancho laughed a gutsy laugh and the guests began to find the comedy in it as well.

"I bet he had a hard time finding directions, maybe he'd get luck from a drowsy bum: 'O-of course, three blocks do-own and take a left...or right, it's a great hotel!'" Otto stated, grinning big, his whole face wrinkling like an old shirt crumpled on the floor.

"Now don't make too much fun of Bolivians. I haven't even started with Germans." Pancho raised one of his eyebrows as he stared at Otto with a smirk on his face, "He didn't have to be drunk to kill all those people."

"Hitler vas a genius..." Otto tried to quench his appetite, but was cut off.

"I mean for goodness sake he killed himself on his wedding night—in a bomb shelter!" Pancho shook his head in disgust. Hans was ready to jump in and stop Otto, but surprisingly didn't have to.

"Vell, no one can counter the truth." Otto said, settling back into his hammock and rolling his cold bottle of beer across his forehead.

A warm breeze blew through the open hallway. Juan passed back his tea gourd and sat silently in his seat shuffling dirt around with his broken shoes.

"So tell me son. You seem like a smart boy. What brings you around these places?" Pancho asked, and not getting an immediate response continued, "You said you were from Santa Cruz, right? That's quite a ways off." He set his first bottle of beer on the ground and opened the next, sending the bubbly foam all over the floor.

"Right, I left Santa Cruz yesterday in a caravan traveling to Paraguay with products to trade." Juan felt puzzled and his head was swimming with pictures, "But we got...attacked." He breathed deeply and looked up for someone to understand him.

"Drug dealing," Pancho supposed quietly. Juan nodded with shame.

"I was forced into the job by my father, and it wasn't my intention..."

"Ve're not against you, son" Hans comforted, "Ve've all done things ve aren't proud of. And that isn't all that bad. Believe me."

"You cannot imagine the pain I felt over and over by shooting innocent people. Reloading and doing it all again, day after day, like a bad dream. It haunts me to this day." Otto bit his dry lip and looked at the trees shimmering in the distance, "They all knew it was coming—they veren't even afraid anymore. I vas the one afraid."

"I'll never forget the look in a young boy's blue eyes after my Lieutenant shot him square between the eyes," Hans added. Juan just looked at his feet. "He kneeled perfectly still for almost half a minute, it could've been a century, looking right through me, it seemed. Then he crumpled like paper in the rain and onto the ground." Hans said, pausing after every word in pity, "I vill never forget that face."

Again the air seemed to go stiff as cardboard and everyone looked down at the ground until Pancho finally asked, "So how did you escape?" Juan looked up and answered,

"We were running away from some guys with guns and a person from our group, Lucho." Hans squinted his eyes and looked on, listening, "While racing away, the person driving the car I was in, Guillermo, took a corner too fast and we somehow ended up crashing. I got out before I really knew what was going on." Juan moved the dirt around with his shoes and after a long pause explained, "I ran as hard as I could until I finally found their house." Juan ended his story and passed back the *poro* to Pancho.

"I'm so sorry, Juan, I didn't know, and I almost..." Otto apologized, sitting up.

"Forget it, Otto," Hans offered.

"It's all right," Juan nodded.

Their conversation was odd, dark, and broken; with so many pauses one would think it was a funeral. But it was an honest conversation. Something the common man doesn't usually have time to share. These are conversations that go on for hours on end because they can, and everything is said without being held back. But oddly enough, silence tells the most many times; it sheds light on things inexplicable, with emotions blazing straight from our souls.

An extremely long pause followed as every person's heart went out to each of the other people around the circle. And so a bond formed between the young and the old. It was not until a couple more *poros*, a few more beers, and some fresh breeze that the conversation picked back up.

"This may seem awkward, but I was wondering, what type of car were you in?" Pancho said, breaking the silence, his eyes flashing.

"A..." Juan scratched his head and thought hard, "A red truck. A four by four, with no back part, you know, with no roof on the back part of the truck."

"A pickup truck, sure," Pancho exclaimed, trying hard not to look overly excited.

"Vhat do you have in mind, Pancho?" Otto asked.

"Well the news is out that a *hacienda* nearby has acquired a prize bull from Argentina worth, I don't know, maybe worth five thousand dollars."

"Five thousand dollars? Who?" Hans asked, leaning way in.

"Don Mililani, a rich senator from La Paz. He owns a whole lot of land down here and is planning to continue to improve his enormous herd." Pancho explained.

"Vhy not just use artificial insemination, it is so much better." Otto said, puzzled.

"It's about prestige, you see, although there are a few benefits of having your own bull. But hey, it's his money!" Pancho laughed.

"So you ar' thinking of having us go and get this bull and sell it to you?" Hans asked, looking at the big picture.

"Precisely, then I could ship 'em off to Santa Cruz and re-sell him." Pancho said winking at the boy with a big smile, "We'll split the profit, like usual." Hans and Otto both nodded in agreement.

"So what does it have to do with the truck?" Juan asked.

"It has everything to do. Unless you want to walk a one-thousand pound bull some ten miles to my place." He chuckled.

The boy half-heartedly accepted the proposition to show them where the truck was. So Hans decided it would be best to pull the stunt off that night after dark. It turned out that the bull was going to be taken to a prestigious bull show in Argentina in the morning. The other reasons apparent were because many guards would likely be off duty because of the upcoming Christmas holidays. And of course because there was a full moon to work with; and with this in mind the group of three promptly set out without lunch to complete the task at hand. Everything was perfectly laid out.

Chapter Fifteen

The sun was steadily sinking down in the horizon, and so was the idea that the truck could be found. Long, dark shadows spread their arms across the dry earth and millions of mosquitoes came out to play in the hair of the trees, while looking for what they loved most—blood.

"Juan, it is novhere," Hans gasped, stopping to look around as sweat dripped off of his chin like a faucet that hasn't been properly turned off.

"Who knows, they could've taken the truck," Otto replied, leaning heavily on a walking stick to hold up his exhausted legs.

"Vell, if vhat Juan saw is right, then it vill be here. You had better be right…" Hans replied, wiping the sweat off of his face and flinging it onto the ground.

"I think we need to look on the road if we are to find it," Juan stated, "I don't know where I am in all these brushes."

"Ha! You get out on the road then you will really be lost, they are all the same, all straight, boring, going nowhere." Otto said, leaning up against a dead cactus.

"No. You know vhat, since you vant to go so badly, let's go," the other aging man said, pointing the way towards the nearest road, "But ve can't look for long because ve've got to go home before dark, and these mosquitoes are *killing* me!" he swatted a bug on his back and hopelessly shook his legs. The boy followed behind looking around in every direction in case he saw that red four by four between the mingling branches.

"Juan! I think I see your footprint again!" Hans said, inspecting a miniature ripple in the red dirt. Otto rushed over to inspect it. The three of them again trudged along, with backs bent low to the ground looking for the next footprint.

"There it is!" Juan exclaimed, pointing to the red truck barely showing above the thick undergrowth. The boy was the first to run toward it, and as he looked for a way to get around the bushes, he stopped and covered his mouth and nose with his shirt.

"You'll be all right," Hans replied as he neared the boy. He put a hand on his shoulder and breathed deeply.

"Vhat is it, let's go!" The oldest man's feet tossed up the dirt as he trudged around the other two and into the bushes. Then he too stopped and stepped back. A multitude of mosquitoes had risen up out of the ground, as the sun began to set, and fresh sweat fueled their passion. But this was not what stopped the group. Several coughs came from Otto and then he said, "You know vhen you get old you lose some of your senses, and I'm always unhappy about it; but vhy didn't I lose my capacity to smell?" Juan crouched over and his stomach undulated, and sent him into convulsions trying to regurgitate.

"It'll be all right, let's just get in there and get the job done before it gets later." Hans encouraged, walking forward into the brush. He came around and found himself looking straight at the front of the car. The driver's door was wide open and mosquitoes covered the entire vehicle it seemed.

"Ah, *scheisse*!" Otto bellowed, "Bad smells!" He slowly stood up straight and eventually went to see the truck for himself, "Are you coming, friend?" Juan shook his head in response. More convulsions followed and he eventually sat down on the ground.

Meanwhile the men took a look at the truck. The inside of the truck seemed in very good condition, and the wheel being out of place was obviously fixable—with leather rope. It surprised them when inside the car there was no body, but a few stains of blood and spilled tea. The driver's seat had been laid back, and was covered in putrid black slime.

"Give me that old rag in the bag, Otto," the other man encouraged. In response he put the leather bag around his neck on the ground and fumbled around until he found an old shirt, and tossed it to Hans.

"Uff!" the older man held his lower back as he straightened out. "Oh, good-night!" he winced and continued, "Let's get out of here fast."

"Vell, if you give me a hand, ve vill!" Hans stammered, nodding towards the truck.

Juan slowly walked around the bushes and looked around. The body of Guillermo had obviously been moved out of the car. Someone had obviously tried to rebuild the steering wheel, but it had not been completed for lack of time. The boy, his face pale and eyes strained, found a seat on the ground several yards away from the other men as they attempted to fix the truck. Hans crawled under the tires and felt around. Otto picked up a couple of large rocks and placed them under the supporting metal beam under the passenger door. He then placed an old-fashioned car-jack onto the rocks and began pumping it up, until it slowly began lifting the side of the four by four.

"I'll turn into road-kill if one those rocks slip out," Hans chuckled.

"It von't, but just hope Juan doesn't get smart and give those rocks a swift kick!" Otto replied. Juan laughed, wiping his eyes dry, as he stood up and walked towards the other men. Just then the car balanced back and forth a bit as the jack was pumped up a little more.

"Vow, no, no!" Hans yelled, as the ginger old man, slipped out from under the truck like a bullet.

"You should sign up to be in a Jackie Chan movie!" Juan joked. But the other men just looked at themselves wondering who that was. "He's a... Chinese actor... really fast, good at fighting, and really funny..."

"Like... Charlie Chaplin?" Otto asked, scratching the side of his head, where some hair still remained. Juan nodded in confusion.

The two men worked hard to fix the out of place steering wheel before dark. Once they had the wobbling wheel lying limp about the height of the other wheel, they tied the broken pieces together underneath with rope and instead of bolts they used rusty wire and old chains. After a good half hour, the men were sweating intensely, glittering in the sun, and covered in dark oil and grease. They could not convince the boy to help them out, so he just sat to the side, drawing in the dirt.

The sun lay red like blood on the horizon, mosquitoes began to swarm mercilessly in the millions—everywhere. Juan squinted in the sunlight and his mocha-colored skin wrinkled on his face. Ash-black buzzards rose into the cooling air and began to swarm above them. And two or three at a time would swoop down near the group and come back up balking. Finally one got up the nerve to land near Juan and hopped around on the ground. Its black eyes shined as it stared straight at the boy. He picked up a rock and threw it at the large bird. It fluttered its wings and spread them as it lifted back up into the air. Soon after two more birds landed, now nearer to the boy, about fifteen feet away. He threw another rock at them, and one of the birds flew away, but the other, almost unaltered, just jumped a little bit and lowered his head.

"Get those disgusting birds out of here!" Otto called out, as he sat in the front seat, trying to turn the car on. It rumbled, eventually started, and then shut back off.

More birds landed, seemingly mocking their presence. Juan ran up to the birds and yelled at them to go away. All of a sudden he held his face and fell to the ground like a stone.

"Juan! What happened?" Hans yelled as he ran toward the boy and kneeled down ahead of him. Juan sat shaking like a leaf, as he skidded his feet away from where he fell. He covered his eyes as he wailed, tears streaming from his eyes. Hans tried to reach him, but couldn't grab a hold of the boy. Juan turned to run, but tripped and fell again a few feet away, onto the hard dirt, sobbing.

"Why! Why!" he begged, grabbed his knees and lay crumpled on the ground.

The carcass that was once the body of Guillermo lay open and exposed to nature. It was blistered and split open, pouring out putrid black blood. His skin looked blue in the dying sunlight; his black eyes were open—still and pensive.

"I...I...let's go..." Hans whispered, looking for words. He kneeled down and put his arms around the boy, holding the young boy to his chest. Otto walked up and also began to tear up in fear at the hideous sight.

"*Wh-y-y?*" Juan screamed, breathing heavily into Han's dusty shirt, holding onto his arm as he shook. He laid his back on a rock and looked up at the sky. Stars appeared one by one, creatively filling the purple sky with inspiration, but they were blurred with tears. Black birds flew above, but Juan did not care to follow their sleek movements. Again they landed on the dead body, pecking away, looking for nourishment in the cool night air. Tears streamed down the forgotten roads on the boy's cheeks, falling monotonously towards the earth. Hans got up and walked towards the car, not knowing what to do.

"Come on, friend," Otto offered, stretching out his calloused hand. Juan accepted it, letting himself be lifted to his feet. The old man led him into the truck and gave him a bottle of water. Meanwhile Hans had gotten a shovel and a tarp from the back of the truck. The buzzards that were disturbing the peace left at his presence. He swiftly dug a shallow hole in the dry, gray earth. He placed half of the tarp into the hole and then pushed the limp body of Guillermo onto it, and a legion of mosquitoes followed the body, moving in waves of black in the sunlight. The tired old man tucked the rest of the tarp over the bloodied carcass and then reached for the shovel. He threw dirt over the unfamiliar face and made a tall mound over it. His blue eyes welled up and he whispered softly, "I hope you find a better home... bless you!" He wiped his face with his sleeve and walked away, "Why does everything have to end this way," Hans said under his breath, biting his lip and shaking head at the darkening sky. He got into the repaired truck's front seat and attempted to turn it on. This time it worked. Juan sat in the back seat, with his head between his knees, shivering. Otto had his arm around him, comforting him with silence. Hans put the truck into reverse, plunged out of the shadows, and drove into the disappearing sun.

Chapter
Sixteen

What of the butterfly that flutters by,
What cares does it carry?
Aside from its joyful life
And vibrant colors—
None.
What of the leaves clapping their hands,
Where is their hope?
In the arms of their strong towers,
Built on the ancient roots
Beneath.
And the salmon of water, to sea, to water;
Who knows their purpose to survive?
To bring life to yet another
And to become dust

nobody

On the vast ocean floor.
But what of this race in their sorrow and hate!
What is our life?
Pursuing dreams that will fall
Like sand castles under the full moon.
Why fight so furiously?
That in our despair to live
We find death.

"Ve don't have to do this," Hans whispered, as he crouched in the shadows of a low tree. Lights reflected in his eyes as he looked at a small house nearby. "It doesn't seem right anymore." Otto shook his head in the corner,

"You're right," he whispered. His fingers shook, as he held a shotgun across his chest, drenched in cold sweat.

"Let's just go...home," the other man pronounced, clenching his fists, showing his white knuckles. The boy put a hand on his shoulder,

"We've come this far, shouldn't we finish this?" Juan persuaded his eyes still red, as he pulled his dark hair out of his eyes, "I mean, what could happen?"

"No, I don't think so, ve'd better go, its' been very long day already," Hans replied, slowly getting up. He took a last look at the enormous bull tied up to the fence, lying down on the dried grass. Its' maroon hide glistened in the moon, stretched tight over its' muscular body. A couple hundred yards away there was a small adobe house, with a dim light coming through its' only window from a kerosene lamp. Hans turned around and began going back to the truck parked in the bushes behind them.

"*Down!*" Otto blurted just as several men walked out of the house they were observing. Hans fell hard on his knees and winced, but kept quiet, proceeding to lie down flat on his face. One of the men walked towards them and stopped not fifteen meters away. He pulled out a cigarette and lit it. Light-silver ribbons flowed from his mouth as he exhaled the deadly smoke slowly and gazed at the sky. The other three men proceeded to start up an old Toyota Land Cruiser. They begged it to awaken, and it moaned, shaking every bolt on its' green hull. The man in the driver's seat expertly turned the key back and forth, while slowly letting on some gas, and in a roar it broke into a grinding rhythm.

"Ricardo, *vamos*!" the three men called as they rode by the other man. He took in a long draught of smoke, burning his cigarette to almost nothing. He tossed it onto the ground and combed his long black hair back as he walked over and jumped into the passenger seat of the small truck. It skidded its back tires and bolted down the dusty road. The bull, suddenly awakened, bolted up and thrust his body at the sturdy fence which he was tied to, his body and eyes burning red in the headlights of the four by four.

"All right, drive the truck around Otto—slowly!" Hans waved over.

"Are we still gonna steal the bull?" Juan whispered, following Otto towards the truck.

"I thought it's vhat you vanted?" Otto asked, patting the boy on his head.

"But…" he tried to find an answer, but Hans waved them back,

"Get to vork," he scanned the area for people, there was still a dim light on in the small house ahead, but it sounded vacant, "Ve don't know how long they'll be gone. And vith a bull like that sitting around you can guess they'll be back soon." Otto, with the headlights off, drove back out of the underbrush and crawled onto the dirt road. Hans got up slowly, rubbing his knees as he walked towards the bull. The moon's brightness shone everywhere, in full glory, encompassed by the stars blinding each other in far away places.

"He's enormous!" Juan cried once Otto had parked the vehicle next to the fence. A large bronze ring dangled from the animal's nose, and he shook his head to keep flies from his eyes. He stomped his feet and rammed the gate with his ivory horns.

"Now, now there," Otto said, holding out his hand to stroke him. Hans reached them and pulled open the gate to the bed of the truck. He pulled out several coils of leather rope and tossed a couple to Otto.

"Here, Juan, come over here," the younger of the men called. He placed Juan in between the fence and the truck, "Stand here, like this, vith your arms out, and vave them like crazy, that vay the bull von't bolt out."

"But if the bull runs at me, I can't stop him!" Juan gasped, putting his arms down.

"Ha! I vould think the same, but in truth the bull is afraid of you. All the animals that I know of are scared of humans," Hans said in reassurance.

Juan squinted his eyes, and shook his head. "What about bull fights?"

"He's not talking about threatening them; it's a kind of rule. If you don't bother them they von't bother you." Otto put his thoughts into the conversation as he untied the bull from the post. Hans was right there, tying a complex knot around the bull's neck in order to control him better. The boy watched as he waved his arms in a circle like he was told to do. Otto ran to the gate and opened it up wide. The boy scooted down to be directly between the end of the gate and the bed of the truck.

"That's it Juan, keep it up and don't get scared away," Hans reassured. Meanwhile he tugged on the bull to move. But his trunk-like legs didn't budge. The other man pulled with the other rope on the other side, but still no progress. Finally Hans whipped the bull on the back, and in the back of the legs, causing it to bolt forward in pain. The small boy immediately backed away, and helplessly waved his arms at the bull; Otto was almost thrown off of his feet as the bull nearly trampled Juan, who threw himself out of the way. The enormous bull reared onto his back legs, and stumbled backwards. Otto regained his composure and pulled the bull down onto all fours.

"You're okay—okay," the old man breathed short breaths, and as he pulled; the enormous mammal struggled to get free. Juan got up, shook the dust off himself and moved in front of the bull and waved his arms again, making him turn to face the truck. Hans, who had fallen in the event, stood back up and led the bull forward.

"How are we going to get him onto the truck's bed?" the boy asked, once the bull had been calmed.

"Vell, ven I worked on a farm in Germany we used to have large ramps, but here I've learned to do it like *this*!" at that Hans hit the bull hard behind the back legs, and caused it to launch forward, just barely putting its' front hooves onto the tail of the car. Again he hit the animal behind the legs, and it stumbled forward, eventually falling onto its front knees. But Otto pulled on his neck and the bull forced himself up jerking the car up and down, again and again. The enormous animal lifted its back leg up and managed to pull himself onto the truck, the other leg following right after.

"There ve go!" Hans yelled, as he followed it up and began to rope up its' back legs. The two old men worked together, tying the bull's legs together so it couldn't move, then onto the sides of the truck. Then they pushed on the middle of the animal's legs, forcing it onto its knees and finally onto its stomach. They expertly tied the animal down with more rope, securing him to the back of the truck.

"Vow, I'm exhausted!" Otto exclaimed, as he wiped his forehead and flung the salty water onto the ground below. A soft wind blew on them as the old men jumped off of the back of the truck.

"That feels nice!" Hans bellowed, stretching his arms upwards. He got into the driver's seat and the other two got in as well. He turned the red truck on and with the headlights still off, drove towards the adobe house to go back to their house for the night.

"I'm very ready to get home and sleep," Otto groaned, breathing deep. The bull lay silently in the back, tired of fighting. "Ve will have to get the vodka out!"

"What is Voud-ka?" the boy asked.

"V-o-d-k-a," Otto replied, spelling it out, "It's a strong drink; I'll let you try some."

"I don't know about that!" Hans laughed.

"Hey, there is a fire up there, where did it come from?" Juan noticed. A small fire was slowly growing right across from the adobe hut, rapidly growing in intensity.

"It vasn't here before…" Otto remarked, as he looked

around. Just then a young man walked around the adobe house, rubbing his eyes. He noticed the red truck and then the fire and shook his head.

"What is going on here?" he questioned, raising a small black box to his mouth.

"Ve saw the fire and vanted to help…" Hans offered, calling to the man.

"This is private property… wait, what is in the back of your…" he spoke into a black box quickly now, "You'd better come over here *boss*, some strange people are…" and that was his last word. Black smoke arose from the end of Otto's trusted shotgun, as its' sound rang out through the plains. The disfigured body of the young man, fell against the wall and slid down to its' final resting place. His innocent eyes shone in the moonlight as Otto pulled the empty shotgun cartridge from his gun, and refilled it.

"Stay in the truck," Hans ordered. Hans, the one driving, got the car in gear, put on his headlights and flew down the dirt road in the other direction the green four by four had gone.

The once small fire grew into a flaming ball of heat, thriving off the dead grass all around. Not long after, the old truck, slowed down at the sight of the blaze, and the group of men got out of the truck shaking their heads.

"I told you, *compadre*—those little buggers will kill you someday!" one of the men joked.

"What buggers, eh?" he pushed the other man away, as he stood before the bright fire, already burning out near the center, but growing outwards in a sort of circle. He pulled a box of cigarettes out of his pocket and hit it against his wrist.

"Those buggers, you moron!" another man, younger and smaller, said, pointing at the pack of cigarettes in the man's pocket. Ricardo turned around and stared him down. He pointed his thumb behind him,

"Stop the fire." He lit a cigarette and took a long puff.

"Ricardo, come and look!" he pointed at the dead carcass of the young boy they had left behind. His body looked like a dying fountain, his blackened blood drizzling slowly down his shattered chest.

"No. *No!*" Ricardo yelled, kicking the dirt and dubbing his tanned skin dome, "And where is the bull, eh? That's why we're here—where is the *bull*?" He smacked his worker in the jaw and ran towards the fence.

"Not there, boss, the rope is gone..." the man said, regaining his confidence.

"My brother! They shot him! Wake up, wake up..." the youngest man blubbered, holding the dead boy's hand, begging for a response. He picked up the body and held his brother's head to his chest as his eyesight was blurred with pain and hate.

"Son of a..." Ricardo bit his lip and walked up to the green truck. He pounded his fist against the hood of the car, "I know who it was. That greedy bastard is going to get hell." Soon the old truck was roaring down the road again.

Chapter
Seventeen

Imagine all the pain you have ever felt and put it into a moment. Now think of all the pain the world is feeling at this moment. Try and capture the pain of the whole world, all it has felt from its design and all it will feel before it dies. It helps you fathom, truly, the burden that life brings—one breath at a time, with every breath. Close your eyes and imagine all of this, in this moment. It's like drowning, losing all hope, and the light fades as your screams become but spheres rupturing in the ocean's waves. And to think that every death, every sorrow, brings another pain as well. It is our curse: the curse of pain.

A green lizard, small and helpless, poked his head out of a corner, and skirted across the opening to a rock, and hid behind it. The black pools filling his eyes, observed its surroundings. Again it darted into some bushes further along. A gang of dogs erupted, as they pursued the creature into the brushes.

"A toast for my friends!" Don Pancho pronounced, raising his beer into the air, spilling some onto the ground below. The red truck was cooling down in the background, under the full moon. The red bull was eating out of a ripped bag of corn. Juan was sitting on the steps of the house, trying not to fall asleep, nervously pulling his head back up every time it swung down. Otto and Hans weakly raised their cups into the air and nodded. "A grand job, boys, su…perb" the large man intoned, grinning large and drinking down the beverage.

"I am exhausted!" Otto sighed, taking a sip of his drink, "Ve'd better get back to our place right away," Hans agreed, holding his lower back as he leaned down to take a seat on the stairs.

"Go home?" Don Pancho questioned, "Who said anything about that? You're my guests—my *heroes*!" he remarked, thrusting his hand into the air for emphasis, "Each and eve-ry one of you!" He filled his glass back up with yellow liquid and had another drink. He rubbed the young boy's hair as he walked into the house.

"Vell, I guess ve could stay the remainder of the night, being that it's vay past midnight already…" Hans debated.

"Of course. My wife will spread out some mats for you to sleep out here in the cool air with me." He yelled down the outdoor corridor and she appeared with a pile of blankets reaching above her head and began laying them out quickly, followed by her servant.

"Let me help you," Otto offered, reaching for one of the blankets.

Soon enough the last kerosene lamp was blown out and everyone went fast to sleep under the setting moon.

"Hear that, Mr. Ricardo?" one of the young men said hearing a distant barking of dogs. He pointed to the right of them into a thicket. The men had gotten out to look for tracks. They seemed to suddenly disappear.

"Your guess is the best we've got, because I can't remember exactly how to get to that hacienda," the boss replied, getting up from off of the ground where he had been examining the road with the help of his headlights.

He motioned with his hand for everyone to get into the truck. He got into the truck himself, put the stick into reverse and went back some fifty feet before shifting into first and driving over the underbrush. The small green truck rocked back and forth over several rocks and broken trees as they approached Don Pancho's hacienda. The men's eyes were focused, filled with anger. But the youngest man, who had lost his brother, had eyes filled with fire itself. He cocked his long rifle, as he had many times already during the trip to find the ranch. The older man in the passenger's seat checked his pistols and then put them in their holsters. The other man in back prepared two large shotguns for Ricardo and himself. He adjusted the baseball cap on his head as the truck's bare tires slowed to a crawl. They were here for two reasons, to avenge a death, and to retrieve their stolen property. They would stop at nothing to do this.

Juan's baby-face glowed in the last beams of moonlight as he unconsciously jerked his head to get a fly off of his cheek. Everyone else was sleeping, with their blankets pulled tight over their bodies. All the beds were full except for one. The muscular bull was resting in the hay. The soldier was out on his duty, though, even if he was sleep-walking. Otto, in old, dusty clothes, was standing at attention in front of the house—his trusted shotgun in his worn hands.

The dogs erupted in panic at the hidden entrance of the house, barking and jumping up and down at the intruders.

"Shoot them already!" Ricardo yelled from inside the truck, as he waited for the gate to open. The dogs put their paws on the gate and rattled it in defense of their property. Saliva dripped from their mouths as their threatened the unwelcome visitors.

"What if its not..." the young man's voice was lost as he tried to get close to the gate.

"I can't hear you?" Ricardo yelled.

"What if we're at the wrong place?" he repeated, now looking at the tall man driving the car. And in response he yelled back,

"Trust me, shoot them!" A shot followed, one of a shotgun. The sad voices of the dogs, yelping helplessly came shortly afterward as they squirmed in the dirt, their eyes wide open, hearts beating at lightning speed.

All six heads were raised on the hacienda's cool porch, and Hans was the first to gain full consciousness. He picked up his gun from next to the door and yelled:

"Vhat vas that?" he looked around in confusion, "Otto, Otto?" he called out.

"Over here, sir," Otto replied.

"Knock it off—vake up!" Hans said, slapping the older man on the jaw. Another shot rang out a second time, and soon after a third. The young man and Pancho soon had their hands on a couple rifles, and the woman grabbed the boy and ran into the kitchen and closed the door.

"What is going on?" Pancho asked, kneeling down next to the side of the house. The sound of a truck revving its engine quickly had all four of them posted behind the red Ford truck.

"Those are the boys from the other hacienda vhere ve took the bull from!" Hans exclaimed, as soon as he got the first view of the green truck coming around the corner.

"I will *not* go down like this," Don Pancho said, shaking his head firmly. His rifle clicked as the large man finished loading it. He flung the gun onto his back and raised both his arms, "What do you want?" he asked in a loud voice as Ricardo pulled his vehicle within a fifty yards of the other and shut of the engine.

"Where is my bull?" he yelled back, leaving his rifle on his seat. The young man's fingers shook as he lined up Ricardo with his long-range rifle. Hans put his hand on the man's shoulder and settled him; the gun slowly lowered.

"Vait, vait," the old man reassured, whispering into his ear.

"*Your* bull? If you want some cattle I would suggest going elsewhere!" Pancho belted back. Meanwhile Otto had climbed over the fence, next to the bull and was crawling around to get a better shot with his heavy submachine gun.

"Are you challenging me and my boys?" he asked, pounding his chest with his arm. The coming of the sun could be seen, with its light slowly wading through the darkness in the horizon. It was to the side of both groups. As they readied themselves for the imminent melee; all three men with the other speaker were now posted around the edges of the other four-door Toyota.

"Boss, I don't see no bull," the youngest man remarked. His eyes glistened with fear and insecurity. He had crawled under the truck and lined up Pancho's head within his sights.

"Oh, it's there all right. Either way—I never back off of a good fight," Ricardo responded, his eyes dancing wildly. He grabbed his gun and slid behind the truck.

On the other side of the field, the young man knelt down at the end of the truck and took the safety off his gun. Hans, with his back against the truck, away from the opposing group, was loading up his old German pistol with heavy lead bullets.

Juan looked on from a small window, rubbing his shoulders as he stood on a stool. Pancho's wife, standing next to the young boy, also looked out, clasping her hands together tightly and shaking her head, with tears flowing down her face.

"Don't do it, be the *real* man … " she whispered futilely

out the window, looking towards Pancho. She waved her hand, forming a cross over her chest and kissed her hand. Next, she kissed a silver cross that dangled from a chain around her neck. Her eyes closed and her head fell skyward.

"Blow his head off," Ricardo called out to his helper under the car. His hands shook as he also crossed his heart and kissed his thumb. His fingers tingled as he felt for the trigger. He closed his eyes as he pulled it.

Schooo… the air crackled as the bullet was thrust into the air. It shot well wide of Pancho, yet he ducked soon after as the sound reached his ears. Hans turned around and in rapid succession shot at the enemy with his pistol. The young man then took a shot—the bullet bounced off of the truck's door.

Thoook! a shotgun rung out in response from the other side of the opening, as the gun let shrapnel fly into the air, and it rattled on the red pickup's hull. Pancho got up from his crouched position and took a shot himself,

Schooo… his bullet ripped through the air and tore open the front tire, letting all the air out at once. The vehicle fell onto that side and balanced up and down. More bullets raced across the empty gap and filled each vehicle with more and more dents. Don Pancho's servant, in unsteady anxiety and fear, rattled several bullets in and out of his gun's barrel, unable to get the next shot ready. The large shells fell out of his hands and bounced off of his gun into the dirt bellow. He reached down to find it, and moved his fingers feeling for it, leaving himself vulnerable.

"Get up!" Hans cried, reaching for the young man. A bullet ripped through the air and hit the young man in the top of the shoulder, shocking the boy to the ground. Hans backed off and shaking his head, he looked up and let off another round of bullets at the other group. The young man's body convulsed and spit out blood as he lost all consciousness. As he breathed his last, his eyes settled on Hans.

"I'm going out there," Juan said decidedly from inside the house, as he jumped off of the stool. The wife was in a corner with her ears covered, vibrating with fear, but still peeking out the open window. The boy, hunched down, opened the door and crawled toward where he had been sleeping and grabbed the heavy rifle Otto had taught him how to use. He also grabbed his old backpack and slipped it onto his back. He crept back into the house and tried to find a way behind the fence without being seen so he could be of help.

"I'm running out of bullets," yelled the young man under the car, trying to make himself heard above the noise. Ricardo failed to notice, focused instead on reloading his own gun.

"There is a full box under the front passenger seat," another man answered back. The young man got up from under the car and opened the door, lowering his head to find the extra shells. He found the box and put a handful in his pocket. He brought the box out and passed more out to the other men. He hid behind the edge of the vehicle with fury in his eyes, took a handful and stuffed them into his front pocket. He expertly refilled his gun and cocked it for another shot as a bullet glazed next to his knee. He winced, but kept his eyes on the various targets across the way. The old Toyota giving them cover, kept shaking all over, rattled from the impact of the hot metal.

"Aim for the big guy, get him down!" Ricardo called out from the other end. As the young man carrying the box of bullets got up to take a look.

Rat-tat-tat! all of a sudden, a machine gun blasted from the undergrowth next to them. The propulsion hit the older worker and left him mangled on the ground.

"No!" the youngest of the men yelled as he sprung up, with wings, it seemed. He pulled a hunting knife from his belt and bolted into the thicket where Otto was reloading.

On the other side of the crossfire, Juan slowly found his way into the fenced in area, hiding in the shadows. He walked right past the bull, who was becoming restless and boisterous, with bullets and shrapnel flying all around him.

"Hans? Otto? Are you there?" the boy called out from behind the fence, trying to make out the shapes from behind the sturdy wooden fence.

"Juan! Where have you been?" Hans asked, as he reloaded his pistol. Pancho was standing next to him, carefully aiming across the battlefield,

"C'mon baby, c'mon..." he whispered to himself. He finally took a shot and it grazed one of the men in the leg. He fell and shook in pain. "Hans shoot him, *now!*" he yelled and the old man quickly finished loading. He turned around to shoot a row of bullets at the fallen man. All the bullets missed as Ricardo pulled him behind the tire and waited for a break. The shouts that he had heard in the bushes next to him had stopped and to his dismay the youngest man never came back out.

Juan had climbed through the fence and was hiding behind Hans.

"Give me your gun, bud," Hans called. Juan handed it over, and the man checked it, cocked it, and leaned into the bed of the Ford to aim it at the other truck.

Right at the moment the old man was about to let his shot ring out, the sound of an engine revving up could be heard. He stopped and looked on, shaking his head.

"No way! More of theirs?" he cried, squinting to see through the brush to get a glimpse of whatever it was coming, "Scheisse!"

But Ricardo and his helper also looked on in disbelief, "The *Milicos*?" he asked his partner, and he nodded. The crossfire stopped, immediately.

"They must've heard the gunfire…" he agreed, backing away,

"Get in!" Ricardo called out as he desperately tried to start the truck. His eyes were raging with anger and frustration, and constantly getting blurred with sweat. He revved it and revved it until finally it roared, its engine booming as it started to move. Both of its' tires on the left were flat, so the truck was driving sideways. But Ricardo didn't care as he ground it towards the house.

An enormous, dark green truck rounded the corner, loaded with fifteen or more young military men ridding it.

"This is Commander Alvarez, what is the problem here?" the commander called from the passenger side, as he sat on the open window, speaking through a makeshift loudspeaker. Pancho put his gun up and aimed at Ricardo as the truck came close. The man stuck his arm out of the window and waved. Hans lowered the large man's rifle towards the ground,

"You know better than I do, ve don't fight together—ve all fall!" Pancho nodded in agreement. Ricardo pulled his truck right behind the red pickup and got out, his helper jumping out of the other end. A bright light blazed on them just as the four men met up, with the small boy sitting on the fence. They covered their eyes as an enormous light set its eyes on them.

"I repeat..." the commander barked across the loudspeaker as one of his young soldiers held up a spotlight, "What is the problem here? Drop your weapons and report to us." Immediately the soldiers began getting off of the truck. Ricardo suddenly spotted the bull lying behind where he had parked his vehicle. He pointed a finger at the other men, while shaking his head. The light was shut off and the men's eyes seemed to play tricks on them as they saw large spots everywhere in the dimmed light.

"Look," Hans explained, grabbing Ricardo's arm, "Ve are enemies, but vith a greater cause! Ve fight alone, ve all die and they take bull and house and truck..."

"You're right, I understand that," he replied hoisting his gun to his chest and moving the old man's way, "If we stay together we may have a chance to survive..." Fifteen or so men were lined up across from them waiting for orders. They were a hundred yards away, and they could be seen, twitching in anxiety.

"Fight the army? There are too many of them!" Juan exclaimed, looking up at Hans.

"They are but boys, like you, lad," he scanned the opposing force, "We have a chance to beat them, if..."

"But they are the army, the good guys, right? This would be illegal!" the boy cried out, confused. Ricardo laughed as he checked his rifle and knelt down behind his truck,

"They are the worst criminals around!" he snickered, "They don't care for justice, they just stalk *haciendas* and find reasons to take others' things at *any* cost."

"So you mean they want to kill us?" he implored, backing into the shadows.

"Sadly, yes." Hans replied,

"You have a lot to learn about the Chaco, boy," Don Pancho pointed out.

The young army men were waiting anxiously to be let loose, like bulldogs being held back by chains. Their faces were dark and their muscular bodies shone in the rising sun. The commander again lifter his loudspeaker,

"This is your last and final warning, drop your weapons and report to us or we will open fire!" he ordered. At that Hans lowered onto his knees and cocked his rifle. Pancho went by the passenger door and put his back against it as he felt around for bullets in his pocket to reload his extended .22 rifle.

"I only have a couple shots left..." he called out, breathing deeply.

"Yeah I'm almost out as well," Ricardo added, "Do we have more in the truck?"

"No, sir, they got spilled yonder," his helper answered.

"I'm okay for a bit..." Hans said. Don Pancho spotted Juan crouching behind the fence, trembling.

"Juan, go into the house and get us some more ammo and a couple more guns," the boy nodded, getting up quickly as he ran towards the house, "Just ask my wife." The boy disappeared into the dark house.

"This is it boys," the old man called out, "Mow 'em down..." he lowered his head and whispered to himself, "Otto, it won't end like this." He lifted his head and aimed his gun. Hans' eyes flashed with memories, hundreds of pictures, scenes, feelings. The memories of war, and he rekindled the passion that drove him then.

Right next to him Ricardo's helper, eyes red from exhaustion, begged for mercy, "Virgen Maria, save us!" he crossed his heart and aimed his gun as well, "Don't let us die like this."

Words are one thing, actions another, but the truth is undeniable. None of them had ever faced such great odds before. Their common enemy had advanced half the distance and was closing in on them. On command, the military men all loaded their weapons and aimed. But the four men behind the barrier were ready for them.

"Here is some ammo," Don Pancho's wife said, as the slim woman shakily handed the boy several boxes of different bullets, "And some g-guns, there should be some in the closet..." the house was rocked and dishes fell to the ground and broke, as man-made thunder flashed outside, flying from guns on both sides of the field. The boy and the lady raced to the window and peered out. A few young men fell from their crouched positions and screamed as they fell to the ground. Hot metal pounded the shell of the trucks on this side. A yell came out from the owner of the *hacienda* as his leg was hit by a bullet that ripped the muscle on his leg.

"No!" his wife yelled out as she opened the back door and bolted out. Juan followed her out and grabbed her arm.

"Don't go, you'll die," the boy persuaded, holding her

back. She fell to the ground behind the fence right next to the house and strained to see what was happening. Shot after shot went off as more and more of the young men fell until only about half were left. Commander Alvarez was behind them with a larger gun, carefully aiming at the heads of the men behind the trucks. Screams and fearful murmurs came from the young men.

"Aim at their heads!" the commander yelled, trying to get rid of the opposition faster. He let a shot go off and it hit the back of the truck, right under the raised head of Ricardo.

"Hit the commander!" Hans yelled in response, as he gripped his gun with soft hands, feeling victory near.

Suddenly the back of the green Toyota started spitting out smoke and small blades of fire. Soon the whole car erupted into a ball of fire.

"*Run!*" Ricardo yelled, as he backed into the fence and furiously climbed it. His helper ran away from the blaze and behind the second truck. Hans ran on all fours, thrusting his body under the fence. Don Pancho desperately tried to get away, but he fell into the dust. In a nervous convulsion the enormous bull leapt up and broke the rope that held him, galloping into the spiny undergrowth behind the house. The eyes of Juan and Pancho's wife watched, in shock, mirroring the blaze of fire and smoke.

The column of fire reached its arms into the air, as it erupted from within. The gasoline tank in the old Toyota completely exploded, sending melting shrapnel away from itself. The force pulled the fence down and crushed Ricardo's body. The blast filled the air with tumultuous black smoke. The four men were instantly incinerated.

"Pancho!" cried his wife, shock filling her face as she ran desperately straight into the explosion. Several large plastic containers sitting nearby were also burned through and the gasoline in them also erupted into fire. The force and heat, threw the woman back ten meters, flinging her corpse into the burning undergrowth.

After a long pause, Commander Alvarez called out, a smirk broad across his face, "Men," he said, pausing again, "Congratulations!" He brushed his hands off and walked towards the fiery chaos.

Juan had slipped away unnoticed, and untouched, and he was already running through the brush as it ripped at his clothes and skin. His fists were clenched and sweating, his mind racing at supersonic speeds. *What now?*

Chapter Eighteen

Somewhere Christmas lights shine through the icicles in a winter storm. A family sits around a warm fire—it blazes brilliantly on the wrapping paper. Cheerful smiles stretch from ear to ear on the faces of the children at Grandma's house.

Somewhere a group of young boys and girls sing carols in the cool winter air. Their eyes sparkle, their wet lips burst with joy under the silver moon.

Somewhere, far away, in a small church, timid youngsters stumble over the poetry they spent days memorizing, sweating in the hot summer evening. Here, fireworks go off, bursting into the air, and church bells ring. It is under one name that they have all joined; it is for one glorious occasion—Christmas.

Somewhere, but not here, not in this field of blood; here men lay disfigured, bleeding still, one day after the battle. They cannot hear the singing nor feel the warmth of a fire, nor even the see the glory of the sunset. No gifts have been bestowed on them, not even a stone to mark their name. They cannot even smell the decay of their own bones as black, scavenging birds feast upon them, tearing at their flesh and singing in their mocking squawks.

Somewhere, not far away, a young boy crawls under the thin shade of a tree and rests his worn body. His face is speckled with dried blood, and his dry skin is breaking open on his face.

Juan groaned as he tried to get the backpack off of his back. He finally managed to set it between his legs as he slid further back toward the tree, its thorns breaking into his flesh. He pulled a sweater out of it and put it on his body. His body was becoming cold as all sign of the sun disappeared, the world following its monotonous turning.

He took out an empty water bottle and removed its lid. He licked the cap and shook the bottle, savoring each and every drop. He breathed deeply as he felt his grumbling stomach. He put his head up against the trunk of the tree and looked through its branches into the dark blue sky. He opened his mouth, as if to speak, but there was no one to talk to, and nothing to say. His eyes welled up in pain and despair. He had walked for two days straight now—from daybreak the day Otto and

Hans died, until now. He had slept in a small rock cave the night before, and by now his hope to survive past this night was fading quickly as the sun completely disappeared to reveal a naked moon dancing in the sky, among the stars.

"Ouch!" he winced, taking his hand away from the ground where something sharp had rubbed him. Carefully he examined what it was, wondering what the grayish-white sticks were. Juan soon realized what they were, yet it did not faze him, he had seen too much already. He was too exhausted to be afraid of the bones of a human skeleton, partially hidden by the dirt that held it up.

His eyes closed, he was no longer afraid. Instead, he began to think about something that he had not thought about in a very long time. The image of a woman, smiling and dressed in white, was walking toward the little boy. His eyes began tearing up and a smile broke upon his face, his lips shaking with joy. It was Juan's mother. Had he ever actually seen his mother's face? He must have but he could not remember. He wished he had her photo with him, to hold it and look at and touch. Would she have loved him if she was still with him? What would become of him now? He put his arms around himself and squeezed tightly. Oh, how he needed someone's arms to encircle him now—someone, anyone. Would his mother embrace him? Would she cry with him and keep him safe?

A boy should never have to feel what this boy did at that very moment. He *wept*.

He opened his eyes to darkness, and he opened his arms to a brutal cold. He could not take this much longer.

Juan's throat burned and his stomach yearned for something to eat. He looked into his backpack once again and pulled out different bags and clothes, but found nothing. He pulled a pair of shoes out and set them next to him as well as some shirts and a pair of pants. He had looked through the bag several times in desperation, but hadn't found anything. This time, though, he took the entire bag and flipped it upside down onto his lap, trying to catch any crumbs from falling onto the ground. Dirt and fuzz came out, and a white piece of paper. The boy, curious, picked up the paper and looked at it. The title read "Wings of Eagles." It had been the tract given to him by the Caucasian man on his first bus ride to Paraguay. He smoothed the crumples out of it and opened the folded piece of paper. He murmured the words to himself, reading every word carefully:

I used to work at a zoo in Santa Cruz, usually in intense heat. I was in charge of the general maintenance, mostly in the bird sector. I fed and took care of the various birds. I would sometimes put some out on a show, for everyone to observe some of the larger, more magnificent birds, although I have come to find out that every bird is beautiful in its own way. An odd thing happened one night, as my shift went unusually late into the night, while I worked on a broken cage. I was squatting on the floor with my tools, when I looked up and saw one of the most pitiful things I have ever seen.

The most magnificent bird we had, the condor, had its enormous wings spread out in the wind. He was free of his cage, tied up like always. A storm seemed to be approaching and heavy winds blew through the barn I was in, and all the birds chirped loudly, waking up from their slumber. But this bird was wide awake. It soared into the air until its chains, which were attached to its ankle, pulled the beautiful bird crashing to the ground. It struggled to get back onto its feet, after hurting itself on the ground as it finally managed to get back up, and it perched once again on the log. And then it tried it again, failed, and tried it again. It did this long into the night as I did my work. It was absolutely pitiful.

Life comes and goes, and in its shortness we are overcome with many questions, yet only a few answers.

But there is one question that sticks out the most, for it is the most important one, "Where will I go after I die?"

The wisest man this world has ever known sheds light on this in his ancient writings, "He has put eternity into man's heart" (Ecclesiastes 3:11, ESV). This man was King Solomon of ancient Israel. He was stating that God created us and has put into every person the knowledge that we will live forever.

Close your eyes: it turns black. Get rid of everything—light, thoughts, all life. Are you now nothing? Could you possibly ever become nothing? Can you imagine that after death you will disappear, cease, stop being in every sense? No. You cannot. It is in our very essence. Tell me otherwise, but you know the truth; we were meant to live forever! In a sense we are like this condor that came from the high Andes Mountains. We are this condor as it gazed up at the stars and felt the wind tugging as it spread its wings. It was meant to fly! We are meant to live forever!

But now another question is left unanswered,

"I will live forever, but where?"

We have two choices, and two only—to live with God, or without him, forever.

There was nothing that the condor could do to be set free, yet every night he tried, but the chains wouldn't break, not by his strength.

We have been tied down as well, ever since we were created, by heavy chains. It was sin, the curse we have brought on ourselves and we cannot get rid of it. "For all have sinned and fall short of the glory of God" (Romans 3:23, ESV). *Nothing we do will please God; we can only be set free.*

"For God so loved the world, that He gave his only Son, that whoever believes in him should not perish but have eternal life" (John 3:16, ESV). *His Son is Jesus. He has broken the chains of sin, and he will break our chains if we only ask him, out of the realization of our hopelessness. He did this out of his love, Christ himself died on a cross to pay for our sins and make us perfect before his Father so we can live with him. Not only does he love you though, he likes you, everything about you, your failures, your talents, he enjoys your joy, yet grieves when you cry.*

All you have to do is see the chains of sin, realize you can't get rid of them alone, and beg for mercy from God's son—the only way to reach God and be with him, forever. God wants you to be with him, he created you, and all that separate you are the chains you carry. All that separates the condor from his family and the free wind are the chains.

Take this gift that was paid for by Jesus Christ for you and you will experience true hope, true joy. You will be given all the blessings that he wants to give to us,

"Even youths shall faint and be weary, and young men shall fall exhausted; but they who wait for the LORD *shall renew their strength; they shall mount up with wings like eagles; they shall run and not be weary; they shall walk and not faint."* (Isaiah 40:30–31, ESV). *That is a promise.*

I did a strange thing that night—I set the bird free and watched it soar into the atmosphere. It never looked back.

Juan let the tract flutter to the ground as he again looked into the sky above. He was exhausted.

In the moonlit night, the stars seem to fade into the background, looking hazy and unknown. Ash-black bats glide in the cool night air, their eyes scanning the earth for food. Their ivory fangs strike out with lights of their own it seems, piercing the blackness. Yet as the slim bodies of these creature fly by the moon, it shines through clear and one might mistake them for butterflies, waltzing in the wind on a spring day. Thin clouds wrap around the horizon, hugging the jagged mountains in the silence, and not far from where the boy lies, desperate and dying, four or five small wooden houses stand clustered behind a wall of thick trees. Smoke crawls out of the chimney and disintegrates in the breeze. A window is open to let air in, and the maroon curtains radiate the red light from the fireplace inside.

The wind takes us across the dry, darkening plains; a small glow catches our eyes, a large house that has been burnt to the ground, slowly burning into ashes, letting off smoke slowly. A couple of vehicles are outside the house, black and charred by some intense heat. Several bodies lay on the ground, a feast for the birds of the air; their poor bones have no place to lay their heads. Again the wind blows stronger, rushing, breaking across the horizon, carrying us far away. City lights fill our eyes and we are carried into a lonely bar, where a large man sits, drinking shot after shot of tequila. He pulls out his cash and the engraved faces of great presidents of the United States flash into view as he quickly counts his stash. His tired and tense face is the last we see as we are again carried out. A few blocks away, in this bustling city, we rest upon a balcony of an old, beautiful house. An old man has struggled to his feet and as the record plays, he holds his dear wife in his arms, as she sits in a wheelchair, smiling under the tears.

Let us leave, may the wind take us far away, for everywhere I look, I see pain, unbearable, breaking pain that cannot be healed.

The sturdy trees point upward at the blackness, sending us crashing out of the atmosphere, and bursting into nothingness. The moon hides its face from us as we pass it, and the farther we get from earth, the more we don't recognize it. On and on we travel, out of our solar system, into the creative designs of outer space. It shines brilliantly and it seems to speak to me through its colors of the beauty of just being, and of enjoying, not one thing, but everything as a whole. Out here I cannot see my selfishness, greed, hate, pride; but I can see the big picture. I realize that the extent of my life, in its own shade, and its value, in blind eyes, is but a grain of sand in the ocean, a blip in the aerospace, a piece of blue in the heavenly painting. Yet, I have truly found the truth and have been set *free* to soar above all of this, with wings to hold me up. How beautiful are the stars from far up above. I retract my telescope and admire; sitting, listening to the silence.

Author's Note

Go on a bus sometime soon and sit close to someone who interests you. Don't talk to them, just look at them and, without making it obvious, try and decipher what type of person he or she is. Are they quiet or talkative? What are their interests?

I saw a woman this morning, and I asked myself these very questions. What makes her different from the rest of the people on this globe? She was walking her dog, and she seemed to be singing to herself softly. I wonder how many other women, about her age, with that type of dog were going for a walk at that same time?

I ask, what makes a person different, unique or special? Today, on this globe, there are almost seven billion people. Each one has a mind of his own, their own opinion about most things, their own style. More importantly, this person has their own problems, their own pain. Do you care about theirs? You cannot, you have your very own. Every grown person has tasted bitter failure, every person has experienced a tragedy, and every soul has seen their heart bleed.

I am the center of everything I do, for the simple fact that I cannot be in any other brain but my own. Oh, the deception! How many times have you looked around and wondered: *What if I am the only true human on this planet?* Maybe all of it is a piece of majestic comedy and you are at the center, the laughingstock. I feel the same way; it's okay, it's not true. At least you know that there are at least two of us.

Yet the pain doesn't go away, the stress doesn't subside. Deception or none, this is not how it was meant to be. You know it, I know it.

You have a burning question right now, don't you? You might even be angry with me: how could I stop this story with no ending? What happens to Juan? Does he die? Or does he find the houses nearby? What about Lucho, will he pay the consequences for his crime?

The truth is that I don't know the answer. I don't *want* to know. Any author could give this story a happy ending, to wrap it up beautifully in silk and send your heart floating into the horizon. So why did I leave this story hanging, threadbare and falling apart in the end? Some of you may be angry at me. Hold on for a few more paragraphs, please.

A few years ago I made a promise to myself. I will never write for mere entertainment or comedy. I hope these are present, but this is not why I write. Walk down the aisles of any bookstore and you know as well as I do that most of the books you pick up have a happy ending, a resolution. Not mine. The reason I write is the same reason I live: to have you examine your life deeply, if only for a few minutes. To open your eyes to the desperation of man, to set the microscope over our souls and let everyone see how dirty and broken we are. More importantly, I write to give you hope, to set a telescope, not a microscope, on God. I want to give hope to the downtrodden, light in the darkest of places and direction to the weary and tired.

This story is, and it also is not, about Juan and his journey through the Bolivian cities and wastelands. It is also a story about *you*. Everyone is at a different place in life, some people believe in God and live for him, others acknowledge him, others are searching for him, some willingly reject him, while others have rejected him and have decided he does not exist. God is. You either reject or accept him. It is like the wind in the air, it simply is. Trying to say there is no God is like telling yourself that there is no gravity, yet you will not jump off the cliff.

I wrote this book to encourage those who love and acknowledge God, to find him in the small, beautiful things in life, and to enjoy him. More importantly, I wrote this book for those who are searching for direction, groping around in the dark for a light, while tears fall from your eyes. We all put on a good front, a smile, a twinkle in our eyes. Yet, each of us have experienced pain, a broken heart, we have felt the cold knife of a cruel comment pierce our soul. We are a hurting people, but we will not give up and admit that we cannot. We will not stop trying and admit we need help. I wrote *Nobody* because I believe that everyone is a nobody until they become a somebody in God. In my God I am accepted, loved, blessed, and ultimately I have purpose and direction. I wish this for you more than anything else I can think of—that you would have peace and purpose.

God has promised, "you will seek the LORD your God and you will find him, if you search after him with all your heart and with all your soul" (Deut. 4:29, ESV). Let God be your peace, let him be your strength, "Peace I leave with you; my peace I give to you. Not as the world gives do I give to you. Let not your hearts be troubled, neither let [it] be afraid" (John 14:27, ESV).

You ask me to tell you what happened to Juan. I cannot. I could make one up, be creative and soothe your discomfort and appease your questioning. But I will not. It would not be fair to you. Take a second and close your eyes, you are looking out at the dying sun as the dry, sandy earth beneath you begins to grow cold. The wind begins to crawl around you as the sweat begins to dry on your shirt and you begin to shiver. *When will this pain end?* You look out at an empty sky and tears start to fall from your eyes. *What will I do?* Will you grab your knees and fight to stand again? *How much longer must I fight?*

They tell us in classes that we came from a monkey and they show a picture of a monkey eating a banana with a funny smirk on his face. If there was ever a deception, it is this. Now, I love science, don't get me wrong. If there is anything that I love reading, it is books debating the issue of Creation vs. Evolution. But this issue goes far beyond what any scientist wants to acknowledge.

I believe that the Theory of Evolution was created, molded and used, at its heart, to get rid of God. A tool, as a black marker, to blot his name out of every single piece of beauty; to enshrine God as religion and as a mere sense of hope. But why? What was so wrong with God? Is he too antiquated, a simple myth?

At the heart of man is a yearning to be free, for good

and bad. Free from all authority, from all discipline, free from all responsibility and restraint. In the name of science, this country and this world have been given the license to rid themselves of God. With this license family has gone, as well as morality, responsibility, honesty—the foundations of what was once America. So be it. If all it takes is a comical story to be *rid* of God, then so be it. But the heart cannot be silent; it cannot forget its Creator. It cannot forget its eternity. If *this* is your freedom, then you have never tasted it.

Give me my God, or give me death!

My heart screams this and it cannot be quenched. If there is no God, what *hope* is there? A coffin, covered in dirt is your end. You are given a plate to name you, but not to remember you; a place in history, constantly overrun by the next dead person, buried next to you. Why endure life if it does not love you?

If there is no God, you are a nobody. I am a nobody. I would rather be the greatest fool and hold to my God, with all the blood in my veins and all the tears in my eyes, than to believe that I am *alone*.

On the contrary, *with* God, there is hope. And he is here, he is not hidden, he is looking for you. With God, there is design in the beauty, a pure scent in true love, warmth in honesty, a desire for responsibility. There is a reason to live for.

If you do not believe in God, then answer me this: why do you still fight for life? Why does death scare you so?

My friend, life is much too short to be wandering for the length of it. This life was not meant to be spent gaining possessions and titles that will vanish forever under the weight of the dirt over your coffin. But there is hope; find True North, find your direction, find God.

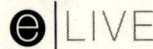

listen|imagine|view|experience

AUDIO BOOK DOWNLOAD INCLUDED WITH THIS BOOK!

In your hands you hold a complete digital entertainment package. Besides purchasing the paper version of this book, this book includes a free download of the audio version of this book. Simply use the code listed below when visiting our website. Once downloaded to your computer, you can listen to the book through your computer's speakers, burn it to an audio CD or save the file to your portable music device (such as Apple's popular iPod) and listen on the go!

How to get your free audio book digital download:

1. Visit www.tatepublishing.com and click on the e|LIVE logo on the home page.
2. Enter the following coupon code:
   8b65-667e-ab6b-8756-8fdb-c065-2860-016f
3. Download the audio book from your e|LIVE digital locker and begin enjoying your new digital entertainment package today!